"Like it or not, you belong to me!"

Rian clasped the ruby bracelet around her wrist as if he were shackling a slave.

"You don't own me, Rian," Laurie flashed. The fire of the rubies struck sparks off the diamonds on her fingers. "You can't buy me with expensive jewels. I don't want them!"

"I don't believe you," he sneered cynically. "Greed is part of every woman's nature."

"Only the women you've known," she replied bitterly. "They probably realized that expensive presents were all you could give. A man without a heart is incapable of giving love."

His eyes flared with anger. "Skip the prim, idealistic speeches. It was your deceit, your pretense that forced us into this engagement. And there's no way I'm going to release you from it!"

JANET DAILEY AMERICANA

ALABAMA—Dangerous Masquerade
ALASKA—Northern Magic
ARIZONA—Sonora Sundown
ARKANSAS—Valley of the Vapours
CALIFORNIA—Fire and Ice
COLORADO—After the Storm
CONNECTICUT—Difficult Decision
DELAWARE—The Matchmakers
FLORIDA—Southern Nights
GEORGIA—Night of the Cotillion
HAWAII—Kona Winds
IDAHO—The Travelling Kind
ILLINOIS—A Lyon's Share
INDIANA—The Indy Man
IOWA—The Homeplace
KANSAS—The Mating Season
KENTUCKY—Bluegrass King
LOUISIANA—The Bride of the Delta Queen
MAINE—Summer Mahogany
MARYLAND—Bed of Grass
MASSACHUSETTS—That Boston Man
MICHIGAN—Enemy in Camp
MINNESOTA—Giant of Mesabi
MISSISSIPPI—A Tradition of Pride
MISSOURI—Show Me

MONTANA—Big Sky Country
NEBRASKA—Boss Man from Ogallala
NEVADA—Reilly's Woman
NEW HAMPSHIRE—Heart of Stone
NEW JERSEY—One of the Boys
NEW MEXICO—Land of Enchantment
NEW YORK—Beware of the Stranger
NORTH CAROLINA—That Carolina Summer
NORTH DAKOTA—Lord of the High Lonesome
OHIO—The Widow and the Wastrel
OKLAHOMA—Six White Horses
OREGON—To Tell the Truth
PENNSYLVANIA—The Thawing of Mara
RHODE ISLAND—Strange Bedfellow
SOUTH CAROLINA—Low Country Liar
SOUTH DAKOTA—Dakota Dreamin'
TENNESSEE—Sentimental Journey
TEXAS—Savage Land
UTAH—A Land Called Deseret
VERMONT—Green Mountain Man
VIRGINIA—Tide Water Lover
WASHINGTON—For Mike's Sake
WEST VIRGINIA—Wild and Wonderful
WISCONSIN—With a Little Luck
WYOMING—Darling Jenny

DANGEROUS MASQUERADE

Harlequin Books

TORONTO • NEW YORK • LONDON
AMSTERDAM • PARIS • SYDNEY • HAMBURG
STOCKHOLM • ATHENS • TOKYO • MILAN

The state flower depicted on the cover of this book is
camellia.

Janet Dailey Americana edition published June 1986
Second printing March 1988
Third printing April 1989
Fourth printing April 1990

ISBN 373-21901-6

Harlequin Presents edition published January 1977
Second printing June 1979
Third printing February 1982

Original hardcover edition published in 1976
by Mills & Boon Limited

CHAPTER ONE

THE AFTERNOON SUN TRIED DESPERATELY to pierce the hazy smog that lay like a dirty halo over Los Angeles, the City of the Angels. There was nothing angelic about the traffic in the streets, racing about like lemmings on their self-destructive path to the sea. Laurie's cab driver weaved and honked his way through the three lanes of bumper-to-bumper vehicles while she braced herself for the collision that never came. An irate motorist shook his fist at the taxi that cut in front of him and Laurie sank a little deeper into her corner. She knew she could never drive as aggressively as the scowling man behind the wheel, although her cousin LaRaine had no such compunction.

The thought of LaRaine drew a weary sigh from Laurie. Laurie was supposed to have been back at their apartment before noon. Her fiery cousin would be furious with her. It wouldn't make any difference that she had been helping Aunt Carrie, LaRaine's mother, prepare for her women's organization annual charity bazaar. Nor would it matter that it had been her aunt who had volunteered her services as typist without consulting Laurie. No, her aunt had presented it to her as an accomplished fact with a snide comment that someone should get some benefit from Laurie's secretarial course.

Resentment flared briefly in Laurie. Her own parents had been killed in a car crash when she was only seven. Her mother had had no living relatives, which left Paul, her father's brother, with Laurie. She dearly loved her Uncle Paul who was so much like the slowly fading recollections of her father. It should have been an ideal solution for her to come to live with Paul Evans, his wife Carrie and their own daughter LaRaine who was only nine months younger than Laurie. It might have been if Uncle Paul hadn't been so wrapped up in his career and Aunt Carrie hadn't devoted every minute to her only daughter.

As a sensitive seven-year-old, Laurie had been quick to realize that their world revolved around LaRaine. Memories of her aunt's parties where LaRaine was paraded in front of the women who gathered came drifting back. Half the time Aunt Carrie had forgotten to mention Laurie except to refer to her in passing as their "little orphan." The remark hadn't been intended to be unkind, but deprived as she was of the secure world of her parents' love, the constant reminder of her status had hurt. And Laurie had been glad to stay in the background while her vivacious confident cousin occupied the spotlight.

Although she had gone to the same schools as LaRaine, had had an equally beautiful bedroom across the hall from her cousin's, and on the surface had been treated as a member of the family, Laurie had looked forward to her high school graduation. Against the wishes of both her aunt and uncle, she had used the last of her father's money to take a secretarial course and thus have the means of earning her own living without being dependent on what had become the charity of her relatives.

There had been a few months of sweet success with money she had earned herself in her pocket every week. Then beautiful LaRaine was out of school, intent on taking a trip to Hawaii. LaRaine was an adult. She wouldn't consider letting her parents accompany her and they wouldn't consider allowing her to go by herself. The compromise was that Laurie should go with her. Feebly Laurie had attempted to protest, knowing her position in the typing pool of the large firm could be filled by someone else at a moment's notice. But the look in her aunt's eyes had plainly said that Laurie owed it to them to give up her job—after all, they had raised her. Laurie had given in, the yoke of forced gratitude bowing her head.

After Hawaii it had been something else, finally culminating in LaRaine's demand to have an apartment of her own. It was a request that was fulfilled after Laurie had agreed to live there, as well. Any display of rebellion by Laurie was always met by the same reproachful looks that reminded her of the everlasting gratitude she owed, with an added, "How lucky you are not to have to work for a living." A bitter smile flitted across her lips. She was a companion to her cousin, provided with room and board and a clothing allowance, at the mercy of LaRaine's whims and the dictates of her aunt. She was twenty-one—without a life of her own or friends of her own.

"This is it, lady," the cab driver growled over his shoulder.

With a start Laurie realized that the taxi had stopped in front of the luxurious high-rise building that housed her apartment. A quick glance at the meter sent her rummaging through her purse for her wallet. The grimace on his face when she handed him the money intimidated her into adding another bill to the tip she had thought adequate. He waited impatiently while she fought the door handle, knowing that if LaRaine had been sitting here she would have ordered the cab driver to open the door for her. But Laurie finally managed it on her own, sending a breathless, "Thank you" over her shoulder as she crawled out of the backseat.

Inside the lushly carpeted lobby with its many urns of potted foliage, Laurie was greeted warmly by the security guard. "Good afternoon, Miss Evans."

"How are you today, Mr. Farber?" she returned in equally friendly tones.

"Just fine, miss," he nodded.

"I'm running late today." A wry grimace revealed the twin dimples in her cheeks. "My cousin expected me back before noon and here it is nearly three."

"I believe your cousin is out." Noting the look

of surprise on her face, he added, ''She swept out of here about an hour after you did this morning and I'm almost certain she hasn't returned.''

That meant absolutely nothing had been done since Laurie had left. Now that she had returned before her cousin everything would surely fall on her shoulders, so with a resigned shake of her head, she smiled her thanks to the security guard and hurried toward the elevators.

As Laurie walked out of the elevator toward her apartment, she blamed the brief spate of self-pity on the tight, sore muscles in her neck and shoulders, her reward for sitting in front of a typewriter for nearly six solid hours. Her future wasn't bleak. There was a bright spot not too far away. LaRaine was engaged to be married and the tentative wedding date was only four months away. Then she, Laurie, would be free to live her own life as she chose, but she knew the next few months would be hectic.

The sight of dresses, evening gowns and trouser suits tossed over every available piece of furniture greeted Laurie as she walked into the living room of the apartment. A resigned dullness clouded her eyes as she recognized her cousin's helter-skelter method of choosing clothes from her extensive wardrobe to be packed in the empty suitcases set to the side. There was typically no note telling Laurie where LaRaine was going or when she would be back. LaRaine Evans was a law unto herself, answerable to no one.

A moment's qualm shuddered through Laurie as

she considered her cousin's engagement. It had all begun almost two months ago when LaRaine had attended another one of those elegant Hollywood cocktail parties, secretly nursing her childhood wish to be "discovered" and become a famous movie star. Laurie never went. The artificial atmosphere of surface gaiety underlined by malicious backstabbing revolted her. It had been unusually early when LaRaine returned from this particular party and Laurie had still been up. Her cousin had swept into the apartment, her calculating brown eyes glittering with suppressed excitement.

"I've just met the man I'm going to marry!" she had announced.

Laurie had been astounded, too familiar with her cousin's indifference to her most ardent admirers to take her seriously.

"Don't laugh, darling," LaRaine had smiled wryly. "This man is one in a million and I intend to have him."

"I just can't believe you could fall in love with a man you only met tonight." Laurie had shrugged her shoulders in amusement.

"Oh, I haven't fallen in love with him, but he certainly has everything to insure that I do," her cousin had replied, tossing her evening wrap on the back of the couch before she curled onto its cushions looking like the cat that had stolen the cream.

"You aren't making any sense."

"Aren't I?" LaRaine had replied smugly. "You wait!"

Her cousin had refused to discuss it any further, preferring the cloak of mystery to any childish confidences. The following morning had brought a delivery of a dozen red roses with an unsigned note requesting dinner that evening. LaRaine had, strangely enough, been ready the instant the doorbell rang, preventing Laurie from meeting her mysterious caller. Flowers arrived daily after that, and always long-stemmed red roses. Laurie recognized the bold decisive handwriting on the accompanying cards as the same as the first. None was ever signed or bore any outpourings of undying love. The messages were always crisp and concise, thanking LaRaine for the previous evening or making arrangements for another.

It was almost two weeks to the day since LaRaine had made her announcement before Laurie had met the man her cousin's whole world had become centered around. Then it had been quite by accident.

Laurie had just washed her hair and had wrapped it in a towel. Cleansing cream was smeared over her face when the doorbell had rung. Grumbling that LaRaine had probably misplaced her key, Laurie had raced to the door, robed in a red caftan, a castoff of LaRaine's that looked too big for her even in its loosely fitting style.

Without any inquiries as to who might be on the other side of the door, she had flung it open to stare in open-mouthed surprise at the imposing figure framed by the door. The man was over six feet, dressed in an impeccably tailored gray suit that revealed his whipcord leanness while accenting the breadth of his shoulders and the narrowness of his hips. Hair as black as her own hidden locks was combed back from his tanned forehead. The artificial light from the hallway reflected the blue highlights in the thick, slightly curling hair. The arrogant slash of his jawline complemented the aristocratic line of his nose, with strength etched in the powerful cheekbones and the bronzed hollow of his cheeks. The cruel set of his mouth drew her attention for a brief moment before her startled gaze raced to meet the hooded look of his dark, nearly black, eyes.

"Who...who are you?" she had stumbled, unnerved to the point of wanting to shut the door in his face.

Dark brows lifted slightly to let the glimmer of arrogant amusement shine from his eyes. "Is Miss Evans in?" His low voice had the decidedly authoritative ring of a man used to commanding and having other people obey.

"LaRaine?" she had asked stupidly before rushing on, "no, no, she isn't here right now. May I tell her who called?"

His eyes had flicked with merciless thoroughness over her disheveled person. "You are her cousin," he had stated.

The slowly drying cleansing cream had hidden the sudden race of embarrassed pink to her cheeks. Laurie could only swallow and nod that she was LaRaine's cousin.

"Would you tell her that I called and offer my

apologies for not being able to keep our engagement this evening.'' A slender tanned hand reached inside the breast pocket of his jacket and removed a long narrow green velvet box which he handed to Laurie. His voice was tinged with cynical mockery as he explained, ''A gift for Miss Evans.''

In that instant it dawned on Laurie that this had to be LaRaine's mysterious suitor, at least mysterious to her because she had never met him. Her cousin had made many insinuations that the man was extraordinarily rich as well as strikingly handsome. Now that she had met him Laurie couldn't think of him as handsome. Striking, yes. Overpowering, definitely. Masculine, undoubtedly, but there was too much hardness and unrelenting strength in his features for him to be handsome. Yet he possessed a magnetism that couldn't be ignored. Still, he was not the type of man Laurie would ever want as a friend, let alone as a husband or lover. And heaven help her if she should ever make an enemy of him, because Laurie knew with certainty that he would be a dangerous man to cross.

The expensive jewelry box in her hand seemed to catch fire, burning her fingers. Laurie wanted no part of him or anything that belonged to him. Hurriedly she tried to shove it back into his grasp.

''You'd better give it to her yourself, Mr., er, Mr.—'' Wildly Laurie realized that she still didn't know his name.

''Montgomery,'' he supplied smoothly, with an imperious nod of his head, ''Rian Montgomery.''

The name was vaguely familiar, but so flustered was Laurie she couldn't immediately place him. There was a twisted cynical smile curling one corner of his mouth as he refused to take back the gift meant for her cousin. "I don't think it will matter very much to LaRaine who actually hands her the present, you or I. I don't have time to argue the point with you. Please give her my message and—" flicking a finger at the green velvet box clutched in Laurie's hand "—the gift."

Laurie had been left standing in the doorway watching him stride to the elevator. Two hours later LaRaine had returned, furious when Laurie told her of Rian Montgomery's visit, but suitably mollified when she saw the jewelry box. Laurie had tried to explain that she thought LaRaine would have preferred Mr. Montgomery to give it to her himself, but her cousin was already exclaiming over the diamond- and ruby-studded bracelet inside the green case.

"What difference does it make who gives it to me?" she had said, laying the bracelet across her wrist and holding it up to the light in silent appraisal, "as long as it came from him."

That was almost an exact echo of his sentiments. In her own case, Laurie knew she would have wanted to receive the gift directly from the giver, especially something as expensive as that bracelet, which considering the cost, she would probably have refused.

"Well, what did you think of Rian?" LaRaine was studying Laurie's thoughtful expression.

Her impression was not what LaRaine would want to hear, so Laurie chose a middle ground. "He was a bit older than I expected."

"Thirty-five isn't old," her cousin had replied scornfully. The dark eyes had returned to the bracelet. "Besides, he's not only rich and powerful, he's also very well known. There isn't a woman born who wouldn't want to marry him."

Laurie knew one—herself. The man she would marry would be gentle and tender, not someone who would dominate everyone in his presence and bend them to his will. "Who is he?" She still hadn't been able to place where she had heard his name before.

LaRaine had laughed, a throaty, sexy laugh she had practiced until it no longer contained any amusement, although it was pleasing to the ear. "Laurie, you're so incredibly ignorant! Rian Montgomery owns the Driftwood hotel chain, among many other things."

The article in the newspaper had come flooding back to her, touting the news that Rian Montgomery was in town after opening one of his hotels in Mexico and was in the process of negotiating the construction of another in some resort area in South America. Laurie also remembered that he was known for his ruthless manipulation of people, as well as the ongoing string of beauties photographed at his side.

When Laurie had realized it was Rian Montgomery her cousin was trying to steer to the altar, she hadn't given her cousin two pins for her chances. During the weeks succeeding Laurie's meeting with him, there had been more presents, each more expensive than the previous, more dates with LaRaine, one more casual meeting with Laurie where Rian Montgomery practically ignored her existence, and finally the stunning news almost a week ago that LaRaine was engaged to Rian Montgomery.

Her cousin could take care of herself, but Laurie still thought she was making a grievous mistake. The very day after her engagement LaRaine had been in a temper that not even the sapphire flanked by diamonds in her engagement ring could assuage, because Rian Montgomery had refused any publicity regarding their engagement. And more than anything else, LaRaine wanted to be in the spotlight. Laurie had known that he wasn't the type of man to be swayed by stormy scenes or a woman's tears. LaRaine had been forced to comply with his wishes.

The only other tantrum that her cousin had thrown had been when Rian was not present. The day before yesterday he had decreed that LaRaine was to visit his aunt in Mobile, Alabama, while he flew to South America on business. Laurie had a sneaking suspicion that Rian Montgomery knew that without his presence LaRaine would flaunt her engagement to the press and public. In front of him, LaRaine had meekly agreed to the trip, only to storm in anger at the injustice of it after he had gone and Laurie had entered the room.

Rian had left for South America yesterday. La-

Raine had her airline ticket for Mobile verifying her reservation for tomorrow afternoon. Laurie stared at the haphazard array of clothes to be sorted and packed for her cousin's journey. She sighed at the wrinkled piles, knowing most of them would need pressing, and LaRaine's ineptitude with an iron was notorious; she scorched nearly everything she touched.

Carefully Laurie began folding the scattered pieces of lingerie and stacking them into a neat pile in preparation for packing one of the smaller scarlet cases. She knew her selection of dresses, trouser suits, and gowns would not be her cousin's. There was no choice but to leave them until LaRaine returned.

The front door to the apartment swung open and LaRaine glided into the front room, her dark eyes dancing with barely suppressed excitement and her crimson lips spreading into a wide joyous smile. Laurie always felt so colorless when her cousin entered a room, so vibrantly alive and stunningly sensuous. The room could be crowded, yet all eyes would be turned toward LaRaine like moths dancing worshipfully about a flame.

"I have the most glorious news!" LaRaine bubbled, spinning and pivoting about the room like a captivating Gypsy, beautiful dark hair floating around her neck while her flared skirt whirled to allow a glimpse of shapely thighs. "It's fantastic! Absolutely magnificent!"

"What is it?" Laurie asked, fascinated by this sirenlike creature who was her cousin.

After being in constant motion since entering the room, LaRaine stopped, enjoying the suspense that was building around her before she announced, "I'm going to be in a movie!"

Laurie's mouth opened and closed several times as her curious blue eyes stared unbelievingly at the smug expression. "What are you talking about? What movie? How?" she breathed at last.

"Ted Lambert, the producer, cast me today." Her eyes gleamed with diamond brilliance. "I met him at a party last week with Rian and he called me today to test for a part in his new picture. And I got it!" For one fleeting moment all sophistication was cast aside as LaRaine hugged herself with childish glee. "I have almost twenty pages of dialogue. I always dreamed about this."

"When does it happen?" Laurie was so stunned by the news she couldn't think straight. "Where will you film? When do you start?"

"I have fittings for my costumes tomorrow." A graceful hand caressed the smooth column of her throat as her cousin became again the self-assured young woman. "I'll be a princess in czarist Russia. They're going on location somewhere in Europe, but all of my scenes will be shot at the studio. Worse luck!" she finished with a dismissive grimace.

Laurie looked down at the dress in her hand, the congratulatory expression receding from her face. She glanced apprehensively at her cousin. "You're supposed to leave tomorrow to visit Rian's aunt in Mobile."

The back of LaRaine's dark head was turned toward her. "I know," her cousin murmured, her enthusiasm dying as quickly as a flame being extinguished. She spun around quickly, her brown eyes dark and imploring. "Laurie, what am I going to do? It's what I've wanted since I was a child. The chance of a lifetime! Mr. Lambert said I was a natural for the part."

Silently Laurie agreed, seeing the regal fire of a princess in her tempestuous cousin. "Call Rian and explain what happened. Persuade him to postpone your visit to his aunt's." It was beyond Laurie's power to resist this sudden desire of LaRaine's for her help.

There was a petulant droop to her cousin's mouth. "I don't know where he's staying. Even if I did...." She left the thought unfinished as she gazed earnestly at Laurie, seeming to beg for her understanding. "You see, Rian...." LaRaine's sudden loss for words touched Laurie's heart more than any eloquence could have done. "I don't think...he would approve. You know how autocratic he is at times. I...I'm sure he wouldn't like it if I appeared in a film. But, Laurie, I want it so much." Diamond tears hovered on the edge of her lashes. "If...if only there was some way I could do it as one last fling before I...I get married, fulfilling one little dream I've always had."

"Surely there is some way," Laurie murmured, confusion deepening her brilliant blue eyes.

"Ted...Mr. Lambert said they would probably shoot my scenes right away since they're filming that sequence first. He doubted whether it would last longer than three weeks at the outside," LaRaine mused aloud, sinking forlornly on the sofa. A tight laugh tinkled out with bitter notes. "Not much longer than my visit to Rian's aunt."

"Perhaps you could call her and explain the circumstances," Laurie suggested practically, missing the speculative gleam bestowed on her by her cousin.

"And have her tell Rian? Then he really would be angry with me," LaRaine sighed, looking suddenly like a shadow of her former self. "I couldn't feign illness and plead a cold or the flu. Rian might find out and come flying back to see that I was cared for adequately."

A measure of her cousin's sadness transferred itself to Laurie. "It seems the only solution is to turn down the part and carry out your original intention of visiting Rian's aunt," she concluded somberly.

"The only problem with that is I've already signed a contract to appear in the film." The rustle of the chiffon dress lying beside LaRaine sounded like electricity crackling in the sudden silence of the room. "If I don't fulfill the terms, the studio can sue me and daddy."

"Oh, LaRaine, no!" Laurie gasped. "Why did you do it? Why did you sign it without at least thinking over what you were doing? You've placed yourself and your family in a terrible position!"

"You have to understand," LaRaine pleaded, leaning forward to gaze with tear-clouded eyes into

Laurie's expression of displeasure. "It happened in an impulsive moment when I was still pinching myself that I'd actually been offered the part. Before I knew what I was doing, I saw my signature on the contract. Now do you understand my dilemma? I don't want to risk my engagement to Rian, nor do I want to hurt my parents."

As if the whole thing was more than LaRaine could bear, she burst into tears, amazingly looking more beautiful and feminine than before. Tears had no more than dampened her cheeks when they stopped, a look of determination spreading over her cousin's face.

"I mustn't feel sorry for myself," LaRaine declared firmly. "I know I got myself into this mess and it's not fair to ask you to help me out of it. But surely the two of us can think of some solution."

Laurie smiled tentatively in sympathy with her cousin while her shoulders and head moved to indicate the blankness of her mind to find a way out of the intolerable situation. LaRaine rose to her feet and walked to the large picture window that dominated the apartment's living room.

"What I need to do is split myself in half." LaRaine tossed the words half-humorously over her shoulder. "One half could go to Mobile and the other half could do the picture."

"An ideal solution if you could do it," Laurie laughed lightly, needing the levity to break the heavy tension in the air.

Her cousin turned around, staring at her raven-haired relative while a light radiated with increasing brilliance from LaRaine's face. "I think I know how we can do it," she breathed. "I know we can!"

"What is it?" Laurie demanded as LaRaine raced from the window to clasp her hands, transmitting the excitement from LaRaine to her.

"You take my place." Mischief danced brightly out of dark eyes at the aghast expression emanating from the blue ones. "I know it sounds outrageous and impossible, but it could work! I just know it will work!"

"You mean, I should go to Mobile," Laurie swallowed, feeling herself drawn into a whirlpool of her cousin's enthusiasm, "instead of you?"

"It's so simple!" LaRaine exclaimed. "Why didn't we think of it before? His aunt has no idea what I look like, except that I'm a brunette and so are you. Rian told me himself that he hardly ever sees her, so the chance of running into her after we're married will be very slim. She won't be coming to the wedding, which is why I'm visiting her now."

"But Rian will find out about the film," Laurie protested half-heartedly.

"I can convince him that I did it before we were engaged. You know how long it takes to make a film, edit it, and get it out to the theaters. By the time he finds out about it, it will all be in the past. Over and done with," LaRaine declared. "Please, Laurie, you must do it—if not for me, then for daddy."

Laurie could feel herself giving in, surrendering

to the habit of sacrificing her desires to show her gratitude for the people who had brought her up. But the prospect of masquerading as LaRaine frightened her into raising another objection, however weak it might seem.

"I could never remember to answer if his aunt addressed me as LaRaine. I would constantly be looking around for you."

"There isn't that much difference between Laurie and LaRaine," her cousin answered sharply before tempering her irritation. "Tell her Laurie is your nickname. She'll believe you."

"I don't like it."

"Do you have a better suggestion?"

Laurie was forced to admit that she didn't Except for the deception involved, she could find nothing wrong with the mechanics of LaRaine's plan. Laurie never actually said she would do it but the agreement was in her silence. And LaRaine was quick to put the plan into action, keeping up a steady stream of chatter about the clothes Laurie would have to pack, trying to convince her what an adventure she would have. The chilling thought kept returning to Laurie that there would be hell to pay if Rian Montgomery ever found out about this masquerade.

CHAPTER TWO

RIGHT UP TO THE MINUTE she had boarded the plane Laurie kept hoping some other solution would present itself, but the doors had closed and she had been on her way to Mobile, Alabama, masquerading as her cousin LaRaine Evans.

The waters of the Gulf of Mexico were a shimmering deep turquoise in the late afternoon sun as the plane made its approach to land. After checking her seat belt to be sure it was securely fastened, Laurie put a reassuring hand to her black hair, verifying that no loose strand had escaped the shining coil around her head. She had chosen the more sophisticated style to give her the poise she needed to carry out this daring charade. There was barely a crease in her warm apricot traveling suit, but she loosened the knotted scarf that matched the apricot and yellow flowered silk blouse. The soft features of her oval face looked serene and composed, except the deep blue of her eyes mirrored the anxiety that brought a dryness to her throat.

Laurie knew she was to be met at the airport. As the passengers disembarked, she listened intently for her cousin's name to be announced over the loudspeaker. She kept assuring herself that nothing could go wrong. Vera Manning, Rian's aunt, had no picture of LaRaine and, at best, only the sketchiest details of what she looked like. With only the slightest stretch of the imagination, Laurie could fit the description.

The palms of her hands became filmed with nervous sweat as Laurie watched her fellow passengers being met by friends and relatives. She followed the mainstream of travelers to the baggage area, keeping her ear attuned to the loudspeaker. The more time that went by without hearing her cousin's name, the stronger the urge became to take the first plane back to Los Angeles. Tricking an old woman into believing she was Rian's fiancée seemed so deceitfully wrong, regardless of the motives.

Minutes later the assorted sizes of LaRaine's scarlet suitcases were gathered around Laurie's feet. The sapphire ring on her finger felt as cold as ice, condemning her part in this charade. What was she to do now, she wondered anxiously. No one had come forward to meet her. Laurie had no address for Rian's aunt, only the name Vera Manning. The whole plan was becoming more hopeless with each heart-pounding second.

"Pardon me."

A hand touched her shoulder and she turned with a convulsive jerk. A tall, bronzed young man with golden blond hair was smiling down at her. Her blue eyes were wide and frightened as she stared into his handsome face.

"Are you by any chance LaRaine Evans?"

Paralyzing fear robbed Laurie of her speech.

His searching hazel eyes seemed to unmask her even as she nodded a hesitant assertion that she was LaRaine.

"What a relief!" he laughed shortly, extending his hand toward her in greeting. "I'm Colin Hartford. Vera Manning asked me to meet you, but I got caught up in traffic and your plane was already in when I arrived." His manner was apologetic, but matter-of-factly courteous. He was a man quite used to charming his way out of a situation. "I was just going to have you paged when I saw you standing here looking so—" his gaze roamed admiringly over her "—so lost."

High color rose in her cheeks, her guilty conscience knowing that if she had truly been LaRaine she would have looked not lost, but impatiently angry at being kept waiting. A glint of amusement gleamed from Colin Hartford's eyes at the delicate blush in her cheeks. He appreciated rare and beautiful objects and knew he was looking at one.

"Are these your cases?" He politely redirected her thoughts, allowing her to compose herself.

"Yes," Laurie answered breathlessly, wondering if he thought their number too many for only a two-week visit, but LaRaine had directed the packing, supplementing Laurie's scant wardrobe with her own. "I came prepared for any contingency," she explained with a nervous smile.

"You'll find the Gulf Coast climate is quite mild in the middle of February, with a few cool rainy days thrown in so one can appreciate the sunshine," Colin smiled, motioning to a porter to take the luggage. "My car is right outside."

A gentle hand on the back of her waist urged her toward the doors leading out of the airport. Colin ushered her toward a gold Thunderbird parked near the curb. Laurie watched as he supervised the loading of her suitcases into the trunk, idly thinking a golden boy should have a golden car. Now that she was truly committed to carrying out the masquerade some of her tension eased. She was able to smile quite naturally when Colin helped her into the passenger side of the car before he slipped behind the wheel.

"Is Mrs. Manning's home very far?" she asked.

"A few miles outside of the city proper," he answered smoothly, putting the car into gear and driving out of the parking area. He slid a twinkling glance her way. "You'll learn very quickly that she's addressed as Vera and not Mrs. Manning. Any reference to age is a very touchy subject. A person either knows her well enough to call her Vera or he doesn't know her at all."

It sounded as if this aunt was as formidable as Rian Montgomery—not a comforting thought. "Have you known her long?" Laurie inquired.

"My father's estate adjoins hers, which is why I was deputized to meet you at the airport," he explained. "Vera doesn't care for crowds or she would have met you herself. She's quite anxious to meet you, LaRaine. I may call you LaRaine?"

Laurie liked the soft way his eyes regarded her, mildly caressive without being objectionable, and his slow drawling voice was a balm to her jangled nerves. "My friends call me Laurie," she said with a quick breath, wishing she could so easily divorce herself from LaRaine's plans as she did from her name.

"I would be pleased to call you Laurie, too, if you call me Colin."

"Thank you . . . Colin." A genuine smile lighting her face for the first time.

"I must confess," his attention returned to the road ahead of them, "the judge—my father—and I had a bet as to what you would look like." At Laurie's wide-eyed look of surprise, Colin laughed. "You've been the subject of many curious speculations since the great Rian Montgomery announced that he was engaged. Vera had decided he would never marry."

Her hands were clenched tightly in her lap as she tried to appear only mildly interested in the subject, unconsciously twisting the snug sapphire ring on her finger. She must remain calm, she told herself, and not let Rian Montgomery's name upset her. Her name was going to be coupled with his quite often in these next weeks and she must become accustomed to it.

"How do I measure up to your expectations?" forcing a lightness to her voice that she didn't feel.

"I thought you would be a beautiful, temperamental woman with a sensual allure that no man could resist." The brilliant gold flecks in his hazel eyes glinted with amusement, while Laurie thought what an accurate description that was of LaRaine.

"The judge, on the other hand, thought you would be a quiet and retiring woman, submitting yourself quite meekly to the pressure of Rian's thumb."

"A sacrificial lamb," Laurie supplied softly, turning her gaze out the window and thinking how true it was in the respect that she always seemed to be bowing to her cousin's caprices. Although she certainly would never bow to Rian Montgomery. A tiny smile brought her dimples into play as Laurie thought how ironic it was that she had been determined to have no part of the overpowering Rian Montgomery, and here she was pretending to be his fiancée.

"You're hardly a lamb." Colin's drawling voice drew her back. "A beautiful Madonna with a touch of the Mona Lisa, a curious mixture of the serene and the sensual. I believe the judge and I were both right and wrong."

The sincerity of his compliment disconcerted Laurie. She was too used to comparing herself with LaRaine and seeing a pale shadow of the more colorful and exciting peacock. Most of the men she had met were usually cast-off admirers of LaRaine's, or entranced with her cousin the instant they were introduced. It had always hurt to know she was second best, like now, when she was a substitute for LaRaine.

"I think you're too generous with your compliments, Mr. Hartford." Her candid protest came from a realistic appraisal of her own attraction.

"I thought we agreed it was to be Colin," he teased gently. "There's no need to be modest, either, although it's refreshing. That ring on your finger is an affirmation of your beauty. It also solves another riddle."

"What's that?" Laurie seized the opportunity to turn the subject away from any more lavish praise which only embarrassed her since it was so undeserved.

"You know that Rian's parents died when he was in his teens. He was raised by his grandfather and Vera. With his grandfather's death ten years ago, Vera took custody of the family jewels." Unknowingly Colin was filling in some of the gaps in Rian's background that Laurie didn't know, and LaRaine either hadn't known or hadn't thought important enough to tell her. "When Rian flew down one morning a couple of weeks ago to select one of the rings from the family collection, Vera was surprised that he had chosen the sapphire instead of the more traditional diamond solitaire studded with pearls. Only Vera, and now perhaps you, would dare question any of Rian's decisions, but Vera did this time. She said he'd remarked that the sapphire and diamond ring would be more suitable for his bride-to-be. As usual, Rian was right."

"How do you mean?" Laurie asked blankly, inwardly shrinking from the weight of the stone on her finger.

Colin lowered his gaze from another minute inspection of her face to the gleaming, richly blue stone. "No other jewel could match the lovely blue color of your eyes. Oh, yes," he mused softly, "I do see how you've been able to ensnare the elusive Rian Montgomery.''

Playacting. An innocent game of pretend. That was what LaRaine had called it in the security of their Los Angeles apartment. Carrying it out was not at all like their conversations. Laurie hadn't realized how cheap she would feel until she saw how her cousin's intrigue had wrapped Colin so completely in their web of deceit.

"How much farther is it?" Her voice was sharper than she intended it to be, but she couldn't stand any more of this talk of her engagement to Rian.

As she stared out the window at the thinning residential area giving way to pine trees, she wondered how she was going to be able to go through with this deception when she was filled with so much self-loathing only an hour after her arrival in Mobile.

"There's no need to warn me of my place," Colin chuckled, meeting Laurie's confused glance briefly. "I'm fully aware that you're one of Rian's possessions. The thought of confronting him will keep me from making any advances that I might consider in other circumstances."

Laurie realized that he thought her quick change of subject was because she thought he was becoming too familiar. "Oh, I didn't mean that. I'm sorry," she apologized quickly, "I didn't mean to sound rude. I'm anxious about meeting Mrs. Manning, I suppose." That was a half truth. She wasn't anxious. She was dreading it, knowing that Colin's inquisition was nothing compared to what Rian's aunt would probably put her through.

"I wouldn't worry whether Vera will approve of you or not. She's been wanting Rian to marry for years. She'll adore any woman who gets him to the altar." There was a blessed moment of silence as Colin turned off the main road onto a peaceful tree-lined drive in the countryside. "Rian has been very closemouthed about you, but then he is about everything. Tell me, how did you meet?"

"At a party in Hollywood."

"That's a surprise." An eyebrow raised slightly. "Rian has always abhorred those gushy affairs. You don't seem the type who would like that artificial atmosphere, either."

"I don't," Laurie answered honestly, inhaling deeply before plunging into the business of pretend. "Perhaps that was the reason Rian—" how his name stuck in her throat! "—noticed me. We left at an outrageously early hour when he offered me a ride home. He asked me out to dinner the following night, and there you have it."

"Love at first sight, huh?" A statement not requiring an answer from Laurie. "Those two stone pillars on your right," Colin directed her attention through the car window, "mark the entrance to the judge's home. The flame pink azaleas ahead is where Vera's land begins."

"How beautiful!" Laurie murmured, catching sight of the brilliant, flowered bushes.

"We've had a mild winter. They're blooming early this year," he commented idly, "which will make the Mardi Gras week just that more colorful."

"Mardi Gras? Are you going to New Orleans?" she asked as he made the turn into the lane.

"Traitorous words," he mocked severely. "Mobile is the American home of Mardi Gras, where it was first celebrated and still is, but without the publicity that New Orleans receives."

"I didn't know that."

"There are quite a few people who don't. The parades and festivities start this week, so you'll be able to see it for yourself."

Covertly Laurie studied Colin, judging the immaculately dressed man to be no older than his late twenties. Instinct said he would be an entertaining and informative escort to the traditional carnival event. But such thoughts couldn't be allowed, so she shifted her gaze to the numerous magnolias and oak trees scattered over the well-kept lawn. The narrow drive ended in a cul-de-sac in front of a scaled-down version of a brick mansion. Red masonry was contrasted by four white columns rising in front of the main entrance to support an upper balcony, with white shutters flanking the windows on both stories. Flowers were everywhere with tropical profusion, azaleas, roses, and more that Laurie didn't recognize.

From the corner of the house a young girl came gliding gracefully toward the Thunderbird and stopped in front of the steps, a basket of freshly cut flowers on her arm. There was a light golden tan to her skin and her hair was an attractive shade of silver blond. No mention had been made of a female Laurie's age, and she wondered who this youthfully slender girl was.

"Here comes Vera," Colin smiled, getting out of the car and walking around to open the passenger door.

Laurie glanced toward the still closed door of the house looking for the elderly woman who was to be her hostess. There was no sign of anyone but the approaching girl.

"I've been waiting so long," the girl's melodic voice brought Laurie's wandering gaze back to her. "I was beginning to decide I should have gone to the airport with you, Colin, to make sure you didn't spirit her away."

Only at closer quarters was Laurie able to see the betraying lines of age marring the slender throat and crinkling the corners of sparkling light blue eyes. The hair wasn't silver blond; it was silver gray, but styled youthfully with gently curling waves that enhanced the patrician features. All of LaRaine's images of a doddering senile old woman were blown away with the wide welcoming smile Vera Manning turned on Laurie after Colin had brushed his lips against the smooth proffered cheek. A whimsical smile touched Laurie's mouth as she remembered her concern over spending two weeks with an older woman and having staid conversations about Rian Montgomery. Meeting her hostess showed her there was nothing staid and dull about Vera Manning. She exhibited boundless energy and a totally outgoing nature.

"If she'd been anyone other than Rian's

fiancée, I would have," Colin was saying. "But as she is, I brought her safely to you."

A beautifully manicured hand reached out for Laurie's. "I'm so happy you could come, La-Raine," Vera Manning declared with obvious pleasure and sincerity. "You're just as I hoped you would be."

"It was very kind of you to ask me to come, Mrs. Manning," Laurie replied, accepting the warm greeting and knowing she was going to like this woman more than was good.

"Kindness had nothing to do with it," the woman laughed. "The invitation was born from my insatiable curiosity and the desire to meet the girl who's going to marry my only nephew. And I insist that you call me Vera." After releasing Laurie's hand the older woman put her arm around Laurie's slim shoulders and directed her toward the house, ordering airily over her shoulder for Colin to bring in the luggage. "We must have a drink to celebrate your arrival. You will stay to join us, won't you, Colin?"

"You know I would never deny myself the company of two beautiful women, Vera," he chided playfully, following them up the steps with the scarlet suitcases tucked effortlessly under his arms and dangling from his hands.

"How glad I am that Rian had to go on that South American trip," said Vera, squeezing Laurie's shoulders briefly before removing her arm and opening the large front door with its brass knocker. "This is a heaven-sent opportunity for us to get to know one another, LaRaine."

Considering the falseness of her masquerade, Laurie thought Vera was giving credit in the wrong direction. The way her conscience was pricking her, it was more hell-sent.

"Laurie," she corrected quickly, explaining, "my friends call me Laurie instead of LaRaine."

Vera nodded sagely. "Laurie, of course. LaRaine is much too harsh-sounding for someone as lovely as you." They had stopped in the cool hallway that served as an entrance hall, and the silver gilt head turned to Colin. "Take Laurie's suitcases upstairs to the white bedroom."

"You're special." Colin slanted Laurie a knowing look. "That room is reserved for Very Important People."

"She's more than that," Vera corrected, bestowing a warm loving look on Laurie's tensely poised face. "Now she's family. Our best is never too good for those who belong to us."

Laurie would have preferred that Vera had disliked her on sight or mercilessly examined her. Anything rather than this wholehearted endorsement as the future wife of her nephew.

"You're embarrassing the girl, Vera," said Colin, drawing the woman's attention to the pink dots on Laurie's cheeks.

"No, no, really," Laurie protested at the slightly hurt expression on the older woman's face. "I'm not embarrassed. I...it's...it's only that you don't know me yet. And what if you don't like me when you do?'' she asked with a nervous laugh.

"If Rian has chosen you to marry," Vera said reassuringly, "then that's all the endorsement I need."

"Ah, Rian," Colin mocked. "The black paragon himself. Although I must admit that I've always admired his taste in the fairer sex and his uncanny ability to find a quantity of quality."

"Those days are over. Now Rian has Laurie and he won't need all those other woman," Vera sighed before glancing sideways at Colin's bronzed form. "And I thought I told you to take the luggage upstairs." With a mockingly deferential bow, Colin complied with her request. "Excuse me, Laurie," the woman turned back to her, "while I get rid of these flowers and prepare us a drink. Would you like to freshen up or anything first?"

"No, it isn't necessary." Laurie didn't want an opportunity to relax, needing the knife-edged tension to force her to carry through the charade.

"Why don't you wait in the living room then?" Vera suggested, ushering Laurie into a brilliant gold and green room. "Colin will be down in a minute and it shouldn't take me much longer than that."

Cream white walls counterbalanced the rich gold carpeting and the vivid green satin curtains with pale sheer insets. The oak furniture repeated the emerald green with complementing live foliage of lacy ferns and climbing philodendrons scattered throughout the room in colorful planters of green and gold. The ornately scrolled high ceilings were dominated by a classically simple crystal chandelier. It was a bold, vivid room, much like its owner, airy and elegant, bursting with vitality.

The prospect of remaining in this tastefully furnished home in the guise of LaRaine Evans, exposed every day to the trusting and loving nature of Vera Manning, seemed to grow more daunting and distasteful every minute she thought about it. Misery forced a long weary sigh to come from the depths of her soul. Why, Laurie wondered to herself, had she been so gullible and allowed herself to be talked into such a situation? The knowledge that she was enabling LaRaine to fulfill her childhood dream as an actress while maintaining her engagement to Rian and that she was protecting her dear Uncle Paul from a possible suit brought her little comfort now that she was here in Mobile staying under Vera Manning's roof.

"Do you feel a bit more at ease?" Colin spoke from the doorway, his fair coloring completing the perfection of the room. "Now that you've passed inspection?"

"Actually," Laurie walked to a green sofa and sat down, unwilling for a moment to meet his gentle, inquiring gaze until she could slip back into the role of Rian's fiancée, "I'm still a bit overwhelmed."

"Why?" he asked casually, taking a seat in a nearby chair.

"I didn't know what to expect," she smiled weakly. "Rian didn't tell me much about Mrs. Manning. . . Vera. I hardly expected her to be so young."

"Don't tell Vera you expected her to be in her

dotage," Colin laughed. "I think she's found the fountain of youth."

"Age is a taboo subject in my house." Vera appeared in the doorway with a tray of drinks in her hands. A wide smile removed any censure her words might have implied. "I refuse to grow old gracefully. Age is purely relative. It grates my nerves when people say, 'How old are you?' The French put it much more tactfully when they ask, 'How many years have you?' It stresses experience instead of deterioration."

"No one could accuse you of the latter, Vera," Colin stated.

"It's one of my eccentricities," she replied, directing a smile at Laurie. "You'll find I have many."

"I don't quite believe that," Laurie smiled, accepting the iced fruit drink.

"I'm disgustingly old-fashioned," Vera declared. "I still won't fly in a plane regardless of how safe they're supposed to be. I'm a follower of that old saying that if a man was supposed to fly, he would have been given wings. I hate cars and ride in them only when there's no other method of transportation. No, the only two means of travel that I enjoy are horseback riding and walking."

Which was why, Laurie realized, Vera wouldn't be attending Rian and LaRaine's wedding.

"Do you ride, Laurie?" Vera inquired.

"I have ridden," she admitted, since it had been one of the activities at the exclusive girls' school she and LaRaine had attended. "But I'm by no means an expert."

"As well as a swimming pool, Vera has a small stable behind the house," Colin explained. "She rides every day."

"The judge, Colin's father, joins me quite often, and Colin is always welcome, too." A knowing glance was darted toward the golden-haired man studying Laurie with open admiration. "The rare times that Rian is here, he's in the saddle almost constantly."

A few questions from Laurie changed the subject from Rian to the horses Vera owned and into a discussion centered on horses in general. A half hour later Colin rose to leave against a mild protest from Vera that it was still early.

"I know the judge is anxiously awaiting my verdict on your guest," Colin smiled, extending his hand in goodbye to each in turn, holding Laurie's a little longer.

"The two of you must come over for dinner tomorrow night," Vera invited.

"I accept your invitation," he nodded, sending a glittering glance toward Laurie. "I'll look forward to seeing you tomorrow."

"Yes," Laurie agreed. "And thank you for meeting me at the airport."

"That was strictly a pleasure." The flecks in his hazel eyes radiated a golden light over her face.

"He's a marvelous young man," Vera declared after Colin had left. "So charming and kind, like the judge. He's attracted to you, too," darting a teasing glance at the veiled expression in the dark blue eyes.

In other circumstances Laurie knew she would be attracted to Colin as well, but the borrowed ring on her finger was the dictator of her life for the present. She couldn't complicate the situation by becoming too fond of Colin Hartford. Unconsciously she touched the cold hard stone of her ring, drawing Vera's attention to it.

"As much as I adore Colin," Vera continued, a reassuring hand touching Laurie's arm, "I'm glad you met Rian first."

"So am I." A tremulous smile didn't add much credence to her lie.

"You're looking tired," the older woman smiled sympathetically. "Let me show you to your room. You'll want to unpack and shower before dinner. You should have time to rest a bit first. I'm afraid I was so excited at finally meeting you that I quite forgot how tiring traveling is."

Laurie freely admitted that the tenseness and strain was in her face, but not from traveling, from maintaining this pretense of being Rian's fiancée. Meekly she followed the silver-haired woman out of the living room down the wide hallway to the curved staircase leading to the second floor. Gold flocked paper decorated the walls of both hallways, with vases of fresh flowers adding further brightness to the sunshine interior.

"I do hope you'll like your room," Vera said, opening a highly varnished oak door to the right of the landing.

The white room—she had referred to it when Vera had directed Colin to take her suitcases there.

Thick white carpet covered the floor, with the walls also in white. But a richly quilted bedspread of gold satin was on the oak bed, with matching drapes at the windows. Brass lamps flanked the bed with snow-white shades on top. It was elegant without being ostentatious.

"It's beautiful!" Laurie breathed in admiration, walking slowly toward the oak dressing table where fresh yellow roses turned their newly budding petals toward her.

Then the gilt-framed picture on the bureau came into view, washing the color from her face as her knees threatened to buckle. Cold black eyes stared out from an aloofly aristocratic male face. Laurie experienced the same unnerving feeling she had felt the first time she had seen Rian Montgomery. It was as if he was in the room, the jeering set of his mouth condemning her as a fraud, a liar. Her heart stopped beating and the terrible fear swept over her again that he would discover this foolish masquerade and send the world crashing down around her.

"I thought you might like to have Rian's picture in your room." Vera's voice came softly from behind Laurie's left shoulder. "It's the only one I have, or I'd give it to you."

"It's a remarkable likeness," Laurie said weakly, unable to break her gaze away from the totally masculine face.

"Do you think so?" the older woman queried, a mild disagreement in her voice. "He looks so hard and cynical in that photograph, but then," she shrugged ruefully, "in many ways he has become that. Money, power and prestige make a potent combination. When you blend those with a forceful personality like Rian's it becomes easy to understand how a person can become cynical toward life. I know I'm not telling you something you don't already know, but you'd be surprised at how many people like you for what you possess instead of what kind of person you are. My most profound wish has been that Rian would find someone who loved him for himself and not for his money and power. I do believe, my dear, that he has found that woman in you."

"Vera..." Laurie began with a choking knot of pain in her throat. Tears brought an added brilliance to the blue of her eyes surrounded by sooty black lashes.

She couldn't go on with the masquerade. It had to end here and now, before the damage was too great to be mended for LaRaine. But her voice couldn't get through the lump in her throat.

The youthfully attractive silver-haired woman mistook the acid tears burning Laurie's eyes for tears of gratitude at being accepted as a member of the family.

"You don't have to say anything. I understand." Vera hugged Laurie's unresisting shoulders and hurried from the room, her own pale blue eyes filling with happy tears.

The moment of truth was gone, and Laurie was more committed than before to carry out the charade to its inevitable bitter end.

CHAPTER THREE

DURING THE NEXT THREE DAYS Laurie discovered how Vera Manning stayed so youthfully trim. They went horseback riding every morning through the quiet country back roads with Laurie astride a gentle, well-mannered bay gelding named Briar, while Vera rode a spirited chestnut. The weather remained unseasonably warm, so their afternoons were spent in or beside the swimming pool. Being an accomplished swimmer, Laurie thoroughly enjoyed the hours spent at the beautifully designed pool. The aesthetic part of her never ceased admiring the cobblestoned apron with its potted ferns and trees that made the pool so out of the ordinary.

There had been one excursion outside Vera's estate, a rare trip by car with Vera's gardener acting as chauffeur. It was a sight-seeing tour of Mobile, stopping to tour antebellum homes, two of the museums and galleries, a stroll along the Azalea Trail, and a visit to the U.S.S. battleship *Alabama* permanently docked in Mobile Bay. Despite Laurie's protests that she didn't need to be entertained, another outing was planned for next week to Dauphin Island with Judge Hartford and

Colin accompanying them for a picnic on the gulf shore beaches and a walk through old Fort Gaines.

The dinner the night after her arrival had been undemanding fun. Judge Hartford was a tall distinguished man with iron gray hair that was a dignified white at the temples. It had been immediately apparent that he was infatuated with Vera Manning and in part, his affection was returned. Only during the introduction was Rian's name discussed. Colin had been politely attentive to Laurie, but never overstepped the bounds of friendship.

The subsequent days after the dinner, Colin had found reasons to come over, once to go riding with them in the morning and twice to swim. His lighthearted banter helped immensely to ease the tension of constantly being on her guard.

Not that Vera was in any way suspicious that Laurie was not who she purported to be. Quite the contrary was true. And the whirlwind of physical activity that Vera Manning indulged in left little time for idle probing conversations. The introduction of Rian's name in any conversation was always casual, relating to some preference for food or something equally unimportant. No, Laurie's concern was that she would accidentally refer to LaRaine's parents as aunt and uncle or mention that her own were dead. It was more difficult than she would have thought because Vera was the kind of woman she could have confided in. In fact, she invited such confidences by not asking for them.

Laurie couldn't help returning the affection that

Vera bestowed upon her so generously. Her own giving nature longed to give it back tenfold, but she had to hold it in check. Realistically Laurie knew that LaRaine would never be a willing party to any long-term correspondence with Vera. Once this visit was over, Vera would probably never see LaRaine, because if she did she would discover the deception immediately. That must be avoided at all costs. So Laurie had to conceal her growing regard for Rian's aunt. To give her love as freely as she would like would end with Vera being hurt by LaRaine's failure to maintain the bonds of friendship after her marriage to Rian, and Laurie cared too much already for Vera to have that happen.

For the first time in recent years, Laurie found herself being regarded as an individual, not being compared to her vivacious cousin. The total acceptance and admiration, not only from Vera but also from Colin and his father, had brought out a previously unknown sense of self-possession and confidence. It was a new experience that was subtly ego-building, even as she railed against the deception.

This is the end of the fourth day, Laurie told herself as she lay between the white satin sheets of her bed. In another ten days she would be returning to Los Angeles. The bitter taste of guilt reminded her that she would never see these people again. Ten more days of pretending and it would all be over. Her tired muscles silently thanked Vera for being so physically active. Tonight was the first night she hadn't fallen asleep the instant her head touched the pillow. Laurie turned her head to the side, her black hair spreading over the white pillow like an ebony fan. Her dark lashes closed over her blue, pain-filled eyes in anticipation of the sleep that would soothe and restore her raw nerves.

There was a light rap on the door. Because of the nearly totally white interior of the room, it never seemed completely dark. Laurie sat up to switch on the brass lamp beside the bed as the door swung open and Vera walked in, her eyes glittering with excitement.

"Were you sleeping?" she asked.

"No," Laurie shook her head. "Is something wrong?"

"There's a phone call for you." A beaming smile spread across the woman's face, still looking young and alive without the benefit of makeup. "It's Rian. You can take it on the extension by your bed."

"Rian?" Her voice broke as she said his name.

"Yes, he's calling from South America. I've already spoken to him, so I'll leave you to talk to him in private."

Vera waited long enough to see Laurie's trembling hand pick up the white receiver. Her heart was racing at top speed as she moistened her lips several times before finally saying a stammering, "Hello," into the phone.

"Is that you, LaRaine?" The crisp male voice sounded no farther away than the next room.

Her hands were clammy with nervous sweat. She was afraid to answer him for fear he would detect the difference between her voice and LaRaine's. She had no choice, she told herself firmly. She had to bluff it all the way through.

"Yes," Laurie answered, trying to achieve the purring sound that came so naturally to LaRaine. "I didn't expect to hear from you, Rian."

"I became curious as to how you were getting along with Vera and vice versa." Yet there seemed to be little curiosity in his voice.

"She's an absolute darling." Laurie seized on LaRaine's favorite terminology, waiting for the ax to fall on her head.

"The gist of Vera's words was almost exactly the same about you." Something resembling disbelief came across the wire, mixed with cynicism.

"You sound surprised."

"Perhaps I can't quite picture you riding horses and swimming all day," Rian returned.

Oh, lord, Laurie remembered too late LaRaine's aversion to swimming. Her own love of water had led her into an unforgivable mistake. "I can put up with anything if it's only going to be for two weeks," she said quickly. "Lazing about the pool has improved my tan. I'll be a golden goddess when you see me again." She was talking too much. Laurie knew she was talking too much, but she knew no other way.

"Vera said you were in bed when I called. Did I wake you?" His swift change of subject surprised her.

"Yes, yes, you did. I must have just dropped off. I still feel a little groggy. I keep thinking this is a dream," a nightmare was closer, "and I will wake and discover you didn't call at all."

"I guessed you'd been sleeping. Your voice sounds a bit different, like soft velvet." That was a compliment, but it was delivered with marked indifference as if it were only a passing comment. "I'll be turning in shortly myself."

"Are you having a successful trip?" Laurie asked, trying to fill the gap left after his last remark.

"Oh, yes, very successful," he replied dryly. "I suppose I should hang up now so you can get back to your beauty sleep."

"You must be tired yourself," she said nervously.

"You sound concerned." There was arrogant amusement now in the vital masculine voice.

"Of course I am."

"I almost believe you mean that. Since we both seem to be tired, I'll say good night."

"Yes, good night, Rian." Relief tinged her voice with a throaty sound.

"Is that all? Just good night?" he mocked.

Her mind raced, trying to think what LaRaine would say. "There's more I would like to say, but I'd rather do it in person."

"Such as?" he prompted with infuriating calm.

"Such as," forcing a lightness to her voice that she didn't feel at all, "I love you and I miss you terribly."

There was a long silence. Laurie felt sure he

could hear the pulsating beat of her frightened heart over the telephone. "Those are not the words that will give a man a peaceful night's sleep when he's miles away from you."

"They aren't meant to," Laurie replied, inwardly sighing with relief at the answering chuckle on the other end.

"Good night, LaRaine."

"Good night, Rian." Thankfully the receiver clicked on the other end only seconds after her words of farewell were spoken.

A wave of exultation rippled over her as Laurie silently congratulated herself on fooling Rian Montgomery. An intonation of speech similar to her cousin's, the excuse of sleep, and the telephone all combined together had made it possible. She hugged the knowledge to herself as she sank back against the pillow. Deceiving Rian Montgomery brought none of the guilt she usually experienced in her masquerade as LaRaine. Now that the fear of discovery had passed, looking back it had almost been fun.

Sapphire blue eyes gleamed at the photograph on the bureau. Not even the smoldering contempt outlined by the aquiline features could quell the excitement that held her in its thrall, but it did remind Laurie of the fine line she had just walked. She didn't want to think of the consequences if he ever did find out. Before the glittering black eyes could steal the thunder of her triumph, Laurie switched off the light, snuggling into the covers with an elated smile still dimpling her cheeks.

THE FOLLOWING MORNING Judge Hartford and Colin joined Vera and Laurie in a horseback ride over the back roads. Colin was astride his own roan hunter while the judge expertly controlled the mettlesome gray Arabian that was Rian's mount when he visited. After the telephone call last night, Laurie was confident she could handle anything. This new poise added a freshness to her appearance, already enhanced by the slim-fitting black slacks and the black and white striped blouse. The folded band of a white silk scarf held her glistening black hair away from her face, cascading it down her back to catch the warm rays of the sun.

The gentle wind had tousled Colin's golden blond hair as he turned his head to silently admire the girl riding beside him. Laurie tossed him a warm smile, not seeing the answering warmth that leaped into his gaze. She wished they could ride on forever, that this contentment would remain.

"This is an absolutely glorious morning!" Laurie declared, gazing out over the dew-kissed meadows, vibrantly green backgrounds for the rich browns of the tree trunks. "I wish every day could begin like this."

"So do I," Colin agreed soberly, his eyes drinking in her sparkling beauty. She flashed him another smile, noticing how handsome he looked in his tobacco brown riding pants and the matching jacket over his cream yellow shirt.

"I don't believe I've appreciated how vibrantly beautiful you look, Laurie," said Judge Hartford, looking back over his shoulder from his position in front beside Vera. "You make me wish I were Colin's age again."

His teasing comment drew the expected laugh from Laurie. "As handsome as you are, judge," she returned gaily, "you would turn any woman's head regardless of her age."

"That may be," the judge smiled, "but I wish I knew the secret of your radiance this morning."

Laurie was about to credit it to the company she was with when Vera spoke up. "It might have something to do with a certain telephone call last night. Am I right, Laurie?"

The expectant look on the older woman's face forced her to agree. "It had something to do with it," Laurie admitted, her teeth grating as she uttered the partially true words.

"Ah, Rian called," the judge nodded sagely while Colin remained silent. "That does explain it then. There's nothing more beautiful than a woman in love, except one who's on the brink."

"Did Rian mention when he would be back?" Colin inserted sharply.

"No, he only said his trip was successful," Laurie replied.

"Which means profitable," Colin murmured with a wry smile.

"I did ask if he would be back in time for Mardi Gras," Vera commented, bestowing an apologetic smile on Laurie. "But he said he didn't think so."

"Mardi Gras starts this week, doesn't it?" Laurie pounced on the subject like a lifeline.

"Yes," Colin replied. The relief on his face

almost matched Laurie's. "We must make plans for you to attend some of the parades and at least one of the balls."

"I would like that," Laurie agreed eagerly. "Do you suppose we could, Vera?"

"Never fear," the judge declared with a twinkling smile. "Leave it to me, Laurie. I'll convince her it would be a major crime for you to miss our most festive season."

Vera laughed, sounding as if she was going to enjoy the charming assault of the distinguished rider as he cajoled her into agreeing.

"Would Rian object?" Colin asked in a lowered voice, slowing his roan so the two older riders could pull ahead.

"Of course not," Laurie declared with an airy toss of her head. She didn't want his name spoiling her day as it was threatening to do. "It was his suggestion—" order was more correct "—that brought me here. I'm sure he must know that Vera will show me around."

"I was thinking," Colin hesitated, "that his objection might be with me. You are his fiancée."

"And you're a friend of the family." Softening her voice to add, "And my friend, too. I won't allow him to object. Please, don't let's discuss Rian."

If Colin thought her request was strange, he didn't comment, but conceded easily to her wishes with a brief description of the Mardi Gras activities over the next week. Gradually the subject shifted to the man and woman riding several yards ahead of them.

"You coming here has been a good thing for Vera," Colin stated. "Especially if the judge persuades her to attend a ball, which I have no doubt he will, because of you."

"Why do you say that? I haven't noticed anything wrong with Vera."

"These past years she's become somewhat of a recluse, using her abhorrence of cars, planes, and crowds to stay at home. She's let her membership lapse in many of the clubs she belonged to, and only her closest friends have stayed in touch," he explained.

"Vera is so warm and outgoing, that's hard to believe," Laurie murmured. "She's always so active, constantly doing things."

"But never becoming involved in anything except Rian." A corner of his mouth quirked.

Laurie let the name pass. "Vera never discusses her husband. Is he the reason?"

"Yes," Colin nodded.

"Well, go on. Tell me what happened. Does it have something to do with his death? Vera did say he died some years ago," Laurie prompted.

"From what the judge has told me of the early days, it must have started long before that," Colin said, slowing his mount so there would be more distance between them and the riders in front of them. "Charles Manning was from a good family which, like a lot of others, lost its money during the depression. But Charles was a very charming opportunist. As lovely as Vera is now, she was that much more beautiful as a young woman. The judge was in love with her even then. If Charles hadn't come along, I'm sure he would have married her."

"But she married Charles Manning," Laurie sighed, remembering how she had guessed the first time she had seen the judge with Vera that he was in love with her. Her heart went out to the distinguished gray-haired man riding so erectly in front of her, his brown eyes never wavering too long from Vera's face.

"She eloped with Charles Manning," Colin corrected bleakly. "You see, Ian Montgomery, Vera's father and Rian's grandfather, saw through Manning's guise of adoration for his daughter as a means to the family fortune and refused to let Vera see him. I've often wondered if he hadn't been so dictatorial whether Vera would have seen what kind of man Charles was. As a matter of fact, I've always thought that Ian Montgomery could have bought him off, but he wasn't a man to be blackmailed."

"What happened after they eloped? Did her father disinherit her?"

"No, Ian was a man with a great sense of family loyalty, and in his old-fashioned way of thinking, Vera was a beautiful woman without the sense to realize what a mistake she'd made. Once the damage had been done and the marriage was a reality, Ian tried to put Charles to work in the family business. From what I understand, during the first few years of their marriage Charles made a concerted effort to be the family man and business executive he was expected to be. But my father says he was a born philanderer. Before anybody realized what was happening he was having an affair with his secretary. Vera always took the blame for his straying because she couldn't have children. She turned a blind eye to every new mistress and the rest of the family had no choice but to do the same."

"Poor Vera!" The lump in her throat was hard to swallow. Such a life would have broken the spirit of a lesser woman.

"Everyone turned a blind eye except Rian," Colin continued. "I told you that after his parents were killed, he went to live with Vera and Charles who were staying here in Ian Montgomery's house. Rian was fourteen or fifteen at the time. Yet he never attempted to hide his loathing and contempt for Charles Manning. He never understood Vera's constant assertions that she loved Charles despite his less than perfect ways. He must have been a terrible thorn in Charles's side, always taunting him about his mistresses, never caring who was there, even Vera."

"That must have made it difficult for everyone," Laurie commented, while partially admiring Rian for daring to bring things out in the open.

"If Ian hadn't died, it's hard to say how long Charles would have continued with his discreet affairs. Rian was twenty-five at the time, a young age to be handed the reins of a sprawling conglomerate. Perhaps it was the absence of Rian and the death of his grandfather that made Charles so reckless. He began appearing at public places with his women and no longer attempted to pretend his marriage to Vera was sailing along smoothly. In fact he was rarely home, and usually only when Rian was expected." Colin paused, staring off into the quiet countryside before bringing his grim gaze back to Laurie. "One day, a few months after Ian's death, Vera met Rian for lunch. They went to one of the more exclusive restaurants in town, only to find Charles at one of the secluded tables with a young blonde. Vera would have walked on past without acknowledging his presence, but Rian walked right up to the table and grabbed Charles by the collar. Rian damned near beat him to death before they were able to drag him away."

Laurie's gasp of surprise brought a sympathetic glance from Colin.

"The intervention of the judge, Charles's failure to press charges, and the power of the Montgomery name kept it out of the papers, but the tongues of the gossips had a field day with it. Vera filed for separation papers, although her religious principles wouldn't allow her to divorce Charles. She rarely ventured out of the house for two years. Then, when she was beginning to take part in some of the social activities again, Charles was killed in a car crash in the company of a married woman. And the whole scandal was revived again."

"No wonder she never discussed any of this with me. It's a pity that the past can't truly be buried," Laurie sighed. "Vera is too loving a woman to have to carry that burden the rest of her life."

·My father agrees with you," Colin smiled. "And he's a patient and persistent man."

"You would really like to see them get married, wouldn't you?"

"I don't remember my own mother. She died when I was two. Vera is the only maternal figure I've known." His gold-flecked eyes glanced at the youthfully trim woman riding beside his father. "Besides, I'm a sucker for a happy ending. And the judge has been in love with her too many years for me not to want to see that love fulfilled."

"I think perhaps Vera is afraid to fall in love again," Laurie commented.

"I think she was more afraid that Rian wouldn't marry." A frown creased Colin's otherwise unlined forehead. "The judge believes that once you and Rian are safely married Vera might be more susceptible to his persuasions."

"Do you think so?" A whimsical expression played over her face as for the first time Laurie hoped that Rian's and LaRaine's marriage would take place soon.

"To tell the truth, when I first heard Rian was engaged, I thought he might be doing it to please Vera and to have children to carry on the family name. You must remember," Colin said with a half smile, "I hadn't met you yet and I couldn't picture Rian marrying for love. Now I can't see how anyone could help falling in love with you."

The need to dim the ardent glow in his eyes brought an instant protest from Laurie. "Colin, please, I . . . ."

"Don't say it," he interrupted swiftly, a bitter curl to his mouth. "I know you're in love with Rian and are going to marry him. I admit I'm half infatuated with you already, but it will go no further. Friends it will be."

Even if she wanted it to be more, like Colin she would have to be satisfied with a brief friendship.

"Shall we catch up with Vera and your father?" she suggested.

Colin nodded, nudging his roan into a canter, and Laurie followed suit.

CHAPTER FOUR

THE SALTY TANG OF THE BREEZE borne over the Gulf of Mexico mingled with the strong scent of chlorine from the swimming pool. The fiery yellow glow in the afternoon sky was turning the red brown cobblestones into burning rocks, as Laurie climbed out of the pool. Her long black hair was plaited into one long braid down her back where it glistened wetly like highly polished ebony. She turned to watch Colin on the diving board. He looked more than ever like a golden god with his burnished blond hair and the even tan of his body contrasting with the white of his swimming trunks. Expertly he jackknifed off the board, slicing into the water with barely a sound. Swimming the length of the pool underwater, Colin surfaced beside the ladder.

"Aren't you coming back in?" he asked, his hazel eyes flicking over her bikini in its design of large yellow daisies against a background of bright blue.

"I think I'll rest awhile," Laurie replied, a bit out of breath from her exertions in the water. She ignored the large bathing towel lying on the umbrellaed redwood table, choosing to let the sun evaporate the water and cool her skin. "Vera will be out in a minute anyway, and I want to make sure the judge will be over for dinner tonight," she added as she stretched out on the cushioned redwood chaise longue.

"You're a veritable matchmaker," Colin laughed, shaking off excess water as he climbed the pool's ladder to join her in the cooling shade of the trees. "These last couple of days you've come up with an amazing number of invitations for my father."

"All of which Vera has endorsed heartily," Laurie grinned. "I've heard the sound of wedding bells is contagious."

"I have to admit I never thought anyone would be able to persuade her to attend that parade yesterday afternoon. But the judge was able to find a secluded balcony to view it from, so her abhorrence of crowds couldn't be used as an excuse."

"She did seem to enjoy it."

"So did you," Colin commented, toweling himself off briskly before slumping into a chair beside her.

"The evening parade tomorrow night might be a bit more difficult. I was thinking," Laurie said with a conspiratorial twinkle in her eyes, "that we could all go out to dinner tomorrow night, then when it was time to go to the parade, you and I could suggest that they stay behind...alone together."

"That's a stroke of genius!" Colin chuckled as

he rose to his feet. "Which calls for an innocuous celebration drink." Laurie laughed gaily as he took her hand, made a mockingly gallant bow over it before bringing it to his lips. "You're a remarkable woman," he averred.

"Thank you, noble sir," Laurie teased back.

Colin sent a jaunty salute in her direction before ambling toward the house. Laurie leaned back against the bright cushions, a contented smile on her face. The days had passed much more swiftly since Colin had related the story of Vera's unfortunate marriage. Laurie had become so involved with finding ways of bringing Vera and the judge together that her apprehension about masquerading as Rian's fiancée had retreated to the background. It seemed so very important that something good should come out of her visit that she devoted nearly all of her attention to that end. Even Colin admitted she had been successful.

The slight breeze had increased. Now that she was out of the direct sunlight, a shiver danced over her skin. As much as she hated to move from the relaxing comfort of the lounge chair, Laurie rose to her feet, walking over to the redwood table to retrieve the flowered wraparound skirt that matched her swimsuit. The hem tickled the top of her leather thongs to transform her bikini into a haltered hostess gown.

As Laurie was securing the tie, a pair of dark-sleeved arms circled her waist, crossing themselves to cup her breasts. Instinctively she stiffened, gasping with surprise as she was drawn back against a hard muscular chest. Warm breath fanned her neck while a pair of lips explored the sensitive cord, sending a fiery trail of tingling awareness through her entire body.

"So that's what you've been doing while I've been away—twisting poor Colin around your finger," a masculine voice uttered huskily near her throat.

A cold shaft of fear was plunged into Laurie's insides as she recognized Rian Montgomery's voice. It wasn't possible, she told herself. He couldn't be here. He was supposed to be in South America for another week or more. But even as her heart cried that it couldn't be true, her mind acknowledged that it was.

With a sob of panic she turned in his arms, trying to use her body as a wedge to halt his searching caress. He allowed the turn, his head raising slightly to claim her lips possessively. Her hands pushed ineffectively against his chest, fighting the whirling sensation that was going on in her head as he forced her unyielding body to mold to the hard contours of his thighs and chest. The sensual mastery of his kiss was gradually turning her limbs into molten lava until her fingers curled around the lapel of his jacket for support.

When his dark head jerked away from hers, flames of fear and embarrassment consumed her face as her rounded blue eyes stared into the cold fury building in his dark gaze. Her left hand was seized roughly, her wrist twisted to confirm the presence of the sapphire ring on her finger before his accusing gaze mercilessly raked her face.

"Who are you?" Rian rasped out viciously, not relinquishing his iron grip on her wrist that kept her pressed against the muscular outline of his body.

"Laurie," she whispered weakly, trembling at the violent expression in his ruthlessly carved face and the havoc he had made of her senses.

"The tractable little cousin," he hissed sarcastically, the recognition and remembrance of her existence glimmering briefly in the dark fires of his black eyes. "What are you doing here? Where's LaRaine?" he demanded, cruelly twisting her wrist farther until she cried out in pain.

"Please!" Her deep blue eyes pleaded with him. "I can explain."

A muscle twitched near his mouth as he stared down at her contemptuously. She was left in little doubt that no matter what she said it would have little effect on him. With derisive amusement Rian noie the swift rise and fall of her breasts that revealed her inner agitation and panic.

"Isn't this a wonderful surprise, Laurie?" Vera's voice cut the heavy silence that had descended between Rian and Laurie. Rian's wide shoulders effectively prevented his aunt from seeing Laurie's terror-stricken expression.

"You'll never know how much of a surprise it was to her," Rian replied calmly.

His cynical gaze scornfully surveyed her pleading eyes and trembling lips. He released his hold on her wrist, letting his hand move to her shoulders. His dark head bent down to her neck in what probably looked like an affectionate caress from Vera's vantage point, but it was only a ruse so Rian could make sure his command was for Laurie's ears only.

"I'll handle this. Say nothing," he murmured harshly.

His glittering eyes examined her face, noting her silently obedient expression before his arm circled her shoulders and he turned to face his aunt.

"Dear Laurie," Rian put ridiculing emphasis on her correct name, "is overwhelmed to find me here."

"I'm not surprised," Vera smiled widely, mistaking the shimmering sparkle of tears in the blue eyes for tears of happiness. "You were so adamant about not being able to return in time for Mardi Gras when we talked to you on the telephone."

The numbed shock was beginning to subside. Her limbs were still trembling and the firm grip of his arm around her bare shoulders burned her skin. Yet Laurie couldn't understand why Rian hadn't denounced her as a fraud. He surely wasn't going to condone the masquerade and let her go unpunished. Unpunished? Her wrist was throbbing painfully already and Laurie knew there would be marks where his fingers had dug into her skin. Her lips retained the sensation of his scorching kiss. It was not something she was likely to forget very soon.

"I concluded my business much sooner than I

expected," Rian was saying, turning his head to look down on Laurie's raven hair. "The thought of my beloved waiting so impatiently for my return probably had a great deal to do with it."

The jeer in his voice flooded her cheeks with a flame-pink hue. He must have found her humiliation amusing, as he added with a biting chuckle, "Isn't it touching, Vera? My desire to be at her side embarrasses her."

"Rian...." Laurie began her pleading protest with his first name, so accustomed to referring to him that way that she momentarily forgot she had no right to be so familiar. But as she met his glittering gaze, like black obsidian, it promptly and arrogantly reminded her. Her own gaze faltered under the glare of his and she was unable to voice her request for him to reveal her true identity.

Vera seemed to sense Laurie's unease. "Darling, I think Laurie would like to freshen up a bit. Here you've caught her completely unaware, without a smidgen of makeup and in a wet swimsuit," she laughed. "It puts a woman at a disadvantage."

"That's the way I would like to keep her," Rian replied, unwillingly removing his arm from around her shoulders. She took a quick step away, freed at last from the power of his touch. His head tilted arrogantly toward her as he gave her permission to leave. "Run along to your room, Laurie, and put on your shield. We'll see how adequate your defenses are later."

Laurie could only smile weakly at Vera as she retreated hastily toward the house. The hot tears that had been burning her eyes flowed with abandon as she swung open the back door and entered the cool hallway. Her blurred eyes didn't see Colin approaching with a tray of drinks until he called out to her.

"Laurie, you're crying!" he exclaimed with genuine concern. "What's wrong? What happened?"

"Rian's back," she sobbed, then throttled her voice with her own hand. Rian had ordered her to say nothing. Undoubtedly he wanted to do the unmasking. Besides, Laurie wouldn't be able to bear to see the withdrawn expression come into Colin's face when he learned she was an imposter.

"I know," he smiled with relief, guessing as Vera had that she was crying from happiness. "I'm bringing out a tray of drinks to celebrate. Where are you going?"

She wiped the tears from one cheek. "I need to freshen up," she said, using the lie that Vera had offered.

"Lucky Rian!" Colin grimaced playfully as Laurie slipped hurriedly past him to the staircase.

There was really nothing she could say in her defense, she realized as she reached the safety of her room. Nothing that would be an adequate enough reason for deceiving Vera, Colin and the judge for these past days. They had believed her to be what she said, offered her their affection and their hospitality, and she had taken it, knowing all along that she was not Rian's fiancée. How could they not look at her with disgust when they discovered her sham as they surely would?

Only five more days, Laurie told herself bitterly, as she entered the gold and white bathroom off her bedroom and turned on the cold tap. Five more days and she would have been back in Los Angeles with no one the wiser except herself and LaRaine. She pressed a cold cloth compress against her eyes to stem the redness that was marring their blue depths. No, the sin wasn't in being caught, Laurie corrected her thoughts, it was in agreeing to the masquerade in the first place. She had known it was wrong, but she had allowed herself to be persuaded into agreeing. She was just as much to blame as LaRaine.

The cold water had the desired effect of clearing her eyes and bolstering her badly shaken poise. Removing the clasp that held her hair in place, Laurie shook it free from the braid. Deliberately she turned the shower on, stepping under the stinging spray to shampoo the scent of chlorine from her hair and skin while hoping the pelting water would banish the memory of the rough material of Rian's blazer where it had bruised her skin. In truth, Laurie was attempting to postpone to the last possible moment the expected confrontation with Rian Montgomery.

As Laurie toweled herself dry a few minutes later, she realized there was slim consolation in the fact that Rian hadn't revealed her impersonation of LaRaine the instant he saw her. After rubbing her long hair nearly dry, she took heart that perhaps Rian wanted to hear the explanation of her being there before he condemned her completely.

Why else had he not denounced her on the spot? Her comb made slow methodical rows through her silken hair as she pondered that possibility, finally deciding it was the only thing that made sense.

While she applied a deep blue shadow that intensified the brilliant color of her eyes, Laurie bade Vera a silent "thank you" for providing this time to marshal her wits. Rian's presence had been narcotically disturbing, proving a turn of events she hadn't anticipated. The outcome was still in question, she realized, as she applied mascara to her sooty, thick lashes, but now there seemed to be a chance to retreat from Mobile with some of her self-respect. All of it depended, of course, on how Rian took her explanation of why she was here instead of LaRaine and his reason for not disclosing her as an impostor.

By the time she had donned her undergarments and a half-slip, Laurie felt more in control of herself, although still considerably apprehensive about the coming hours. She scanned her wardrobe thoroughly, searching for the right dress to wear. It was true that a woman gained confidence from a well-groomed appearance and Laurie was going to need all she could get.

The knock on the door took her by surprise. "Who is it?" she called out sharply, turning toward the door as it opened and Rian Montgomery walked in unannounced. As Laurie grabbed for the robe hanging on the closet door, she saw his insolent appraisal of her scantily clad figure. Her cheeks were once again set aflame. "You could have waited for permission to enter!'' she flashed, hating him for catching her unaware again.

"When you were swimming, you paraded in front of Colin wearing less than what you have on now.'' His mouth curled into a jeer as he crossed the room to her side with the grace of a jungle panther.

Laurie would have liked to have said that Colin didn't look at her as though she were a piece of merchandise to be pawed, then cast aside if she didn't meet certain standards, but her position was too tenuous for such impertinence.

"I wasn't referring to my attire,'' she spoke with forced calm, "but permission to enter my bedroom.''

"Do I need permission to enter my fiancée's bedroom?''

She met his mocking gaze, pride hiding the pain in her gaze that his stinging words had evoked. "We both know I'm not your fiancée.''

"Everyone here thinks you are. Their glowing words of praise for you are still ringing in my ears.'' The sarcasm in his low voice lashed out at her like a whip, drawing an involuntary flinch. Her gaze fell from his sardonic features to the expertly tailored white slacks molding the firmness of his thighs below the navy blue blazer jacket.

"I'm sorry about that, Mr. Montgomery. I . . .'' Laurie began humbly.

"Oh, please make it Rian,'' he sneered.

She clutched the ivory satin robe tighter around

her throat, faltering for a moment before tossing back her head to send the dark curls cascading down her back. In the depths of her blue eyes there burned a flash of anger which she veiled quickly with her lashes.

"I'm sorry," Laurie repeated more forcefully.

One side of his mouth quirked in derision. "I'm sure you are. My arrival was very inopportune... for you."

"That's not what I meant and you know it." There was a desperate ring to her voice, but Rian only found amusement in her discomfort.

"You don't honestly expect me to believe you're sorry for ingratiating yourself with my aunt." Contempt was sharply etched in the arrogantly inclined head, his tallness making Laurie feel all the smaller.

"You're making this sound like a cheap trick," she protested weakly, her chin beginning to quiver from the turmoil of her emotions. "There was never any harm intended to anyone."

"Would you like to explain that to Vera?" Rian demanded harshly, his nostrils flaring in white-hot anger.

Her oval face turned downward, tears of shame blurring her vision, her eyes fixed on the white carpet beneath her bare feet. It was a silent admission of defeat. It was true no harm had been intended, but what had started out as an innocent deception had reached gargantuan proportions. When Vera discovered who Laurie really was, there would be bewilderment and pain.

"I would like to explain," Laurie murmured.

"No doubt I'll be fascinated by your tale, but not now." He cut her off sharply. Icy disdain embittered his voice. "My romantically inclined aunt touchingly agreed that since we've been separated for so many days, we should be alone this evening."

"You haven't told her yet?" Enormous blue eyes stared at him in disbelief.

"I'll meet you downstairs in half an hour," Rian said harshly, deliberately ignoring her question. "That should give you ample time to fabricate a believable explanation." He took a step toward her and Laurie involuntarily backed up. The curl of his unrelenting mouth mocked her action as he reached behind her into the closet and withdrew a blue jersey dress. "Wear this," he ordered. "It matches your deceptively innocent eyes."

With the backhanded compliment ringing in her ears, Rian thrust the hangered dress into her unwilling hands, then left the room. His departure left her gulping for air, only then realizing how his constricting presence had suffocated her. On wavering legs, Laurie stumbled to the velvet-cushioned bench in front of her dressing table, the repercussions of their conversation raining about her head. She was expected to spend an entire evening with him! An entire evening fielding his sarcastic jibes! Listening to him tear her story apart! Remembering how the masquerade had come about made Laurie realize how unbelievable it sounded, how totally selfish the motives were.

A hysterical laugh rose in her throat. From the outset she had considered the masquerade dangerous, that Rian Montgomery would make a formidable enemy. Why hadn't she listened to her own warnings? There would be hell to pay if Rian ever found out, she had told herself once. Staring at the blue dress in her hands, Laurie knew Rian was going to extract every ounce of payment from her. Fatalistically she realized there was nothing she could do to prevent it.

Exactly half an hour later, Laurie walked out the door of her bedroom, unnecessarily smoothing the clinging fabric of the dress over her hips. The aesthetically pure design of the cerulean dress effectively accented her shapely figure. The simple boat neckline set off the graceful column of her throat while artfully accenting the rounding swell of her breasts. Skillfully tailored darts nipped in the waist, then widened over her slim hips and allowed the silken skirt to curl around her legs.

Her raven hair reflected blue highlights from the dress although it was pulled severely back into a chignon at the nape of her neck. Laurie felt like a martyr walking down the stairs on her way to be burned at the stake. Frantic butterflies beat at the walls of her stomach as she gripped the polished oak banister for support. She wanted to command her legs to carry her away from this house and Rian Montgomery, but she was afraid if she did, she would discover that they would nightmarishly refuse to move.

A door opened near the base of the stairs and Rian walked out, looking darkly compelling in a black dress suit and tie. Yet it made him look no more civilized than a black panther wearing a jewel-studded collar. Laurie froze in the shadow of the stairs, her pulse erratically fluctuating as she waited for Rian to see her. There was another man with him, several inches shorter, with close-cropped brown hair and dark-rimmed glasses. It was the second man who caught the flash of her blue dress on the stairs.

His brown head immediately turned in her direction, a wide smile softening the thin face. "You're looking more beautiful than ever, LaRaine," he called out.

As Rian's dark eyes coldly inspected her appearance, Laurie forced her trembling legs to carry her down the stairs into the light. With quailing heart, she watched the other man's expression change to one of astonishment.

"You aren't LaRaine," he murmured, darting a curious look at Rian's unfathomable expression.

"Surely you haven't forgotten so soon what my fiancée looks like," Rian drawled blandly, moving to the base of the stairs to meet Laurie. The scorching touch of his fingers was on her elbow, firmly leading her to the still gaping man. "You remember my man Friday, E.J. Denton, don't you, Laurie?"

Scarlet color stained her cheeks as she briefly

met the man's incredulous gaze. Numbly he held his hand out to her, mumbling a greeting which Laurie returned with equal embarrassment. The man's puzzled glance returned again to Rian, seeking an answer to his unspoken question, with none forthcoming.

"Get hold of David tonight," Rian ordered crisply. "Tell him I want that report on the Rexler company tomorrow. He can send it by courier if he has to, or bring it himself."

It was an obvious dismissal and it sent E.J. Denton scurrying back into the study. His departure left a fragile silence behind. Laurie was vividly conscious of the man standing beside her, his strong hand still gripping her arm as if he expected her to flee. He wasn't to know that she was incapable of movement. She was trapped by her own conscience that insisted she receive her due punishment for her foolhardy action. Yet her gaze was wary as it rose to meet the enigmatical expression in his eyes.

Once again Laurie was forcefully struck by the strength in his face, so compellingly handsome, at the same time so forbiddingly relentless. The aristocratic lines were stamped with arrogance and the eagle sharp perception of one accustomed to command. If she wasn't so frightened, she would have seen how amusing it had been for her and LaRaine to think they could fool him and get away with it.

"Have you found it yet?" Rian jeered softly, snapping the toothpick silence.

Laurie started visibly. "Found what?"

"I imagine you were looking for my Achilles' heel."

"If you ever had one, I'm sure by now you have it impregnably protected," she declared with surprising sarcasm.

"I'm glad you realize that," he snapped grimly, his fingers digging deeper into her arm in punishment for her biting tone. Then he forcibly turned her toward the front hallway. "My car is outside."

Laurie jerked her arm free of his grasp, tilting her dark head defiantly as she walked briskly toward the front door. She wanted to get the inquisition over with quickly while her pride still maintained a precarious hold on her composure. Her sensitive radar told her Rian was only a step behind her. The back of her neck tingled where his dark gaze surely rested on her. As she reached the oak entrance door, a dark-sleeved arm reached in front of her to open it.

"You two aren't leaving already, are you?" Vera's voice sounded from the living-room door.

Rian's hand touched Laurie's waist, the electric contact halting her when she would have bolted through the open door. Her inner apprehensions had written too much of her agitation in her eyes for Laurie to allow the other woman to see her face.

"I'm afraid so," said Rian, successfully keeping his tall figure between the two women. "We have early reservations."

"I was hoping you could have a drink with us before you left," Vera sighed before her voice brightened. "When you come back, we can get together."

"Yes, when we get back." There was dry amusement in his voice before his hand was removed from Laurie's waist and she was free to walk out the door.

A white Continental was parked in the driveway next to Colin's gold Thunderbird. Laurie briefly thought how much more enjoyable an evening it would be if she were climbing into that car instead of Rian's. But the white door was being opened and Laurie slipped gracefully in, the white leather seat wrapping her in luxury. Clasping her hands tightly in her lap, she stared straight ahead as Rian climbed in behind the wheel. She swallowed nervously, waiting for the sound of the motor starting, only to hear continued silence. A sideways look at Rian found him staring coldly at her, his eyes raking her stiffly controlled appearance.

"Your hair offends me. Take it down," he ordered with autocratic arrogance.

"No!" Her angry refusal was accompanied by a protecting hand moving to the smooth chignon of raven hair coiled against her neck.

Before she could prevent it, rough fingers were pulling the pins out of her hair, raking through it to sent it into a billowing black cloud around her shoulders.

"You don't have the sophistication to carry off such a severe style," Rian decreed, a dark brow arching cynically at the rebellious expression on her face.

"How would you know?" she demanded, regretting her impudence at the answering flash of anger in his eyes. As quickly as the fire in his gaze burst into flame, it was banked.

His hand reached up and flicked the visor down in front of Laurie. He pointed toward the mirror. "Tell me whether you see a poised young woman or an inexperienced girl."

A vulnerable oval face looked back at her, shimmering blue eyes sparkling in a childlike temper. Rian's aquiline features mocked her reflection as the soft curve of her lips drooped with defeat. Her sharp retort had been as effective as the pathetic hiss of a kitten trying to hold a snarling jungle cat at bay.

CHAPTER FIVE

THE RESTAURANT RIAN TOOK HER TO was one of the more plush, exclusive places in Mobile. The evening hour was early and most of the tables were vacant. Still Rian instructed the maitre d'hôtel to give them a secluded corner table where a potted palm insured them of further privacy from the nearest table. A black-suited waiter appeared instantly.

"Drinks before dinner, sir?" he queried.

Rian shot a quick glance at Laurie who was nervously clutching the gold-tasselled menu. "I..." she began, preparing to voice her refusal for any alcoholic beverage. She had never cared for the taste of liquor.

"A Bacardi cocktail for the lady and I'll have a Manhattan," he ordered with a dismissive nod of his dark head.

"I don't drink," Laurie protested as the waiter withdrew from their table.

"You're as taut as a violin string," Rian mocked, taking in the pallor of her face. "A cocktail will relax those knots in your stomach so you can enjoy your dinner."

The condemned ate a hearty meal, Laurie thought bitterly, knowing she had little recourse.

Under his watchful eye, she took an experimental sip of the drink when it arrived. The brightly pink liquid was surprisingly sweet, with the citrus tang of a lime twist floating in the shaved ice.

"Is it satisfactory?" Rian inquired.

"Yes, thank you," Laurie nodded, setting the champagne style glass back on the table. Her blue eyes hesitantly glanced in his direction, noting the languid ease with which he reclined in his chair. If only she could feel so relaxed, she wished.

Trivial conversation was impossible between them and the silence stretched out like an invisible barrier. Laurie had expected the interrogation to begin when they had left the house, but Rian had seemed preoccupied during the drive to the restaurant and although his hooded gaze strayed to her often, there were still none of the endless questions she had anticipated. To fill the awkward stillness, her hand kept reaching for the drink until finally the glass was drained, leaving a pale pink foam around the lime slice. His own drink was barely touched.

The waiter reappeared at Rian's side. "May I order for you?" Rian asked with condescending politeness.

Food was the farthest thing from her mind and Laurie quite willingly left the choice up to him. With the complacency of a man who knows exactly what he wants, Rian gave the waiter their order without consulting the menu. Laurie had believed herself to be too nervous to eat, so it was a surprise when she discovered she had eaten the last of the freshly caught fried shrimp. The before-dinner cocktail combined with two glasses of white wine with the meal had banished more of her tension than she had realized. The dinner plates were removed and a cup of steaming black coffee was in front of her. Laurie was sitting comfortably back in her chair, no longer on the edge of her seat as she had been.

The strike of a match across the table from her prompted a glance at her quiet dinner companion. A pencil-thin cigar was between Rian's fingers, sending a gauzy gray cloud into the air above the table. The knife point in his dark eyes pinned her attention.

"Explain to me how you came to be at my aunt's," his crisp voice commanded decisively.

The period of truce was over. Rivulets of perspiration collected in her palms as Laurie fought to meet his watchful gaze without flinching.

"I don't know where to begin," she murmured helplessly.

His mouth quirked cynically. "The beginning is the usual place. I already know the end."

There was too much strength in his features for Laurie to combat. Her gaze fell to the china cup in front of her. "LaRaine fully intended to come to Mobile. She'd already begun packing to leave when she received a telephone call from Mr. Lambert," she began hesitantly.

"And who is Mr. Lambert?"

"He's a film producer in Hollywood." She glanced up as his gaze hardened with uncompromising severity. "She'd met him at a party you'd taken her to the week before. He offered her a small part in a movie he was producing." Laurie swallowed nervously, unconsciously edging forward in her chair, seeking to impress upon Rian the importance of the opportunity to LaRaine. "You see, LaRaine has dreamed of becoming a movie star since she was a child. So when the offer came, it was like a dream coming true for her. If she turned it down, the chance of her ever being considered again would be just about nil."

"Oh, yes, the opportunity of having a woman's beauty exploited and magnified on the screen is definitely not an offer to be lightly refused," Rian drawled sarcastically.

Laurie blanched, feeling his words were censuring her rather than LaRaine's actions. "LaRaine became carried away by the unexpectedness of the offer. When Mr. Lambert offered her a contract on the spot, she accepted it."

"Only afterward did she remember she was supposed to visit my aunt, is that right?"

"Something like that, yes." The icy disdain in his eyes sent cold shivers down Laurie's back. "She didn't know how to get in touch with you to explain what had happened. The contract was already signed committing her to appear in the movie."

"Is that when the idea of sending you in her place was conceived?"

A weak smile curved her lips. "Actually it started out as a joke. LaRaine remarked that she wished she could be two people—one of her could go to Mobile and the other could do the film.''

"I can take it from there," Rian said dryly, stubbing the cigar out in the ashtray. "But what made you agree to the masquerade? Did you nurture secret dreams of becoming an actress, too, and see that pretending to be LaRaine would give you experience?''

"No," Laurie denied quickly and a bit breathlessly. "It wasn't anything like that. LaRaine was legally committed to appearing in the film and morally obliged to come to Mobile. If she didn't live up the first commitment there was a chance that her parents could become entangled with legal actions. They took me in when my parents were killed. Uncle Paul has a successful business. A suit from a large movie studio could have ruined him,'' she explained earnestly. "At the time it seemed such an innocent thing—to pretend to be LaRaine, considering the damage that could have occurred to my uncle if my cousin had come here instead of fulfilling the contract.''

"Was I to learn the truth when I returned, or was it a case of what Rian doesn't know won't hurt him?'' he jeered, his lip curled derisively as the truth flitted across Laurie's expressive face. "That's what I thought," he ground out sarcastically.

"LaRaine didn't want you to think less of her, and she was afraid you would," Laurie murmured.

"So this little episode was to be kept a secret until after we were married, I suppose." The leashed violence was evidenced by the arrogant flare of his nostrils and the clenched jaw.

"I don't know," Laurie mumbled untruthfully.

"I could hardly be expected to endorse this farce, now could I?"

"No," Laurie agreed numbly, feeling the humiliation wash over her afresh. "You have every right to be angry. But please," she turned the pleading look in her blue eyes on him, "don't blame LaRaine entirely for this. That movie role was sort of one last fling for her before you two were married. She never intended any harm to come of it." That arrogant austere expression on Rian's face frightened Laurie. Somehow she had to salvage LaRaine's engagement that, by the look on his face, Laurie guessed was about to be broken. "After all, it was my idea to come here in place of LaRaine," she lied. "I don't think it would have ever occurred to her to deceive you this way. I convinced her I could do it."

Her false admission was met by stony silence as Rian signaled to the waiter for their check. Now what, Laurie wondered, following Rian's lead as he rose from the table. He surely wasn't going to leave it at that. She had told him how she had come to pretend to be his fiancée. Didn't he intend to tell her what he was going to do?

The tables were nearly filled with elegantly dressed men and women. Laurie noticed the way heads turned as she and Rian walked by, but his presence always seemed to dominate any room. She wasn't aware of the way his masculine dark looks complemented her own quiet, dark beauty or the way her inner agitation had produced a glowing color in her cheeks. Next to Rian Montgomery, Laurie felt very inconsequential.

When they reached his car, he still maintained the silence between them until Laurie thought she would fairly scream. He was doing it deliberately, exactly the same way he had prolonged her explanation. He probably enjoyed seeing her squirm, she thought angrily, casting a mutinuous glance at his sharply defined profile.

The city was being left behind them. Yet Laurie sensed that this wasn't the direction that would bring them back to Vera's home. But she refused to question their destination. It wouldn't do for Rian to know that she preferred the safety of numbers when she had to be in his company. Nervously Laurie thought he had probably guessed that already. Did he know how his hardened reserve intimidated her? Her mind was racing so swiftly, trying to second-guess his motives, that she didn't notice the speed of the luxury car decrease until the sound of rubber tires slowly turning over sandy gravel penetrated the silence.

The cessation of movement followed by the switching off of the engine alerted Laurie to her surroundings. They were parked in a widening of a country road with the dark shadows of the pine woods behind them and no sign of any buildings. A few feet in front of the car were the shimmering waters of Mobile Bay reflecting the silver gold orb of the moon. Across the bay the fairy lights of the

city became lost against the star-speckled sky. A
match flared to life, briefly illuminating his aloof,
arrogant features as Rian touched the flame to the
tip of his slim cigar.

Laurie swallowed nervously, wanting to know
what they were doing here but refusing to ask. A
movement from Rian flooded the dim interior with
jarring light. Pushing the dark curls behind her
ear, she turned to meet his relentlessly searching
gaze.

"Now that you've got yourself into this situation, how do you propose to get yourself out?"
Rian mocked sarcastically.

Her finely arched brows lifted momentarily. So
she was to name her own punishment, Laurie discovered with surprise, before realizing that with a
man like Rian Montgomery a person would never
get off easily. But her own sense of guilt wouldn't
allow her to anyway.

"There are really only two alternatives," she
replied, determinedly keeping the quaking of her
bones from affecting her voice. "I can pack my
suitcases tonight and leave in the morning as
LaRaine Evans. Or I can go to your aunt, explain
who I really am, and how I came to be here."

"And shatter all her precious illusions in so doing," he added grimly.

Her hair fell like a jet-black curtain over her
cheeks as Laurie bowed her head in acknowledgement. "I know," she murmured. The last thing
she wanted to do was to hurt the woman who had
welcomed her so openly and so completely into her

affections. "The most logical thing would be for me to leave tomorrow morning."

"It would be the easiest," he agreed sardonically. "What happens when Vera eventually meets the real LaRaine?"

"She won't...I mean, LaRaine said..." Laurie stammered, "she said you hardly ever see Vera. The chance of you bringing LaRaine here was practically nonexistent."

"I wonder why she thought that?" he remarked indifferently, leaning back against the plush seats with indolent disregard.

"That's true, isn't it?" Laurie whispered. "Vera told me herself that she hardly ever sees you."

"In Vera's terminology, three or four times a year is hardly ever seeing someone." His gaze narrowed on her stricken face. "So what do you propose now? That I cut myself off from any association with my aunt to protect you?"

Laurie sighed heavily, "No, you can't do that. I'll...I'll just have to tell her the truth and hope she doesn't hold this against LaRaine for the minor role she played."

"And everyone concerned is just supposed to forgive and forget that any of this ever happened, is that it?" Freezing contempt glittered in his dark eyes.

"Do you have any other suggestions?" Laurie demanded sharply, tired of the cat and mouse game he was playing with her, wishing that if he was going to pounce on her, he would do it and stop toying with her.

A twisted smile lifted one corner of his mouth. "Yes, I have one. You can stay here as my fiancée and we'll forget there ever was a LaRaine."

"You can't be serious!" Laurie gasped, watching in disbelief as he calmly exhaled a gray cloud of smoke. "You aren't going to let my stupid masquerade break up your engagement to LaRaine! You can't!"

"As far as I'm concerned," Rian stated coldly, "our engagement was broken the day she took off my ring and put it on your finger."

The silver gold band of the sapphire ring fitted snugly, defying Laurie's attempts to pull the burning circle of metal from her finger. Before she could succeed, her right wrist was seized in a vicelike grip that nearly stopped the flow of blood in her hand.

"No, no!" Laurie protested vehemently, struggling uselessly to free herself from his hold. "I can't let you take your vengeance out on LaRaine. She loves you! She's talked of little else but her marriage to you and how much it means to her. All of this was my idea," she repeated, willing to take all the blame on her shoulders rather than see her cousin's engagement broken. "She wouldn't have agreed to it if I hadn't convinced her. She even said she didn't want to be in the movie if it meant risking her engagement to you! You two loved each other. You were going to be married. I can't let you hurt LaRaine because of my stupid plan."

"It's very touching the way you leap to your cousin's defense," Rian commented cynically, not releasing the hold on her wrist that brought his lean hard face so close to her. "But I fear you don't know your cousin any better than you know me."

"What's that supposed to mean?" Laurie breathed. Her blue eyes hesitantly met the enigmatic expression in his nearly black eyes.

"LaRaine didn't love me any more than I loved her." His face glittered with mocking amusement at the astonished and disbelieving expression in her face. "It was a case of satisfying a mutual need. I wanted a wife who was well-bred and attractive, someone who wouldn't demand too much of my attention. LaRaine wanted a rich husband who would buy her jewels, clothes, and offer an opportunity to mingle with the socially élite."

"How can you say that!" Laurie exclaimed in a horrified whisper. "You don't know how LaRaine really felt about you. Not if you believe what you just told me."

"I'm sure it suited the image she wanted to project for you to believe that she loved me." His cynical reply struck a cold shaft of doubt in Laurie. "LaRaine is too much in love with herself. ' Laurie did know LaRaine well enough to know that Rian might be telling the truth. Her cousin could sometimes be very calculating and unfeeling, totally selfish when she went after what she wanted.

"It doesn't change anything," Laurie murmured, lowering her gaze to the lean brown fingers holding her wrist. "If you don't really care for her then it doesn't make any difference whether or not your aunt likes her."

"Vera is incredibly romantic." His low voice

carried a derisive note. "She wouldn't understand why LaRaine would allow you to come here pretending to be my fiancée."

"So you want to keep up a pretense, too?" Laurie snapped caustically, suddenly hating him for being so cold and inhuman. Marriage was a sacred thing to her, not something to be indulged in to satisfy a material or physical need. At the same time, her loathing didn't carry itself on to her cousin who was guilty of the same sin, according to Rian.

"I don't want to hurt my aunt unnecessarily," Rian corrected with cold anger.

But Laurie's slow-to-rise temper didn't pay heed to the warning. "And you propose to prevent that by acquiring me as your fiancée? What happens to her feelings when our engagement comes to an end?"

"Why should it?" His eyes mercilessly raked her face, noting the blue sapphire eyes sparkling with her anger, adding a volatile beauty to her face. "You're an attractive little orphan girl." His words cut her to the quick with the harsh reminder of her lonely childhood. "Surely the security of a rich husband isn't something to be casually dismissed?"

"Money isn't the most important thing in the world to me," Laurie declared proudly. "When I marry, it will be to the man I love and who loves me. He'll be someone tender and warm and kind."

There was a flash of white teeth, indicating a smile, but the expression mirrored in his eyes revealed only disdain for her romantic avowal.

"You speak as though you have someone in mind. I can't believe the love of your life is waiting at home while you're here pretending to be my fiancée. Or is it someone you recently met? Colin, for instance?"

"Colin is all those things," Laurie admitted defiantly, not caring whether Rian thought she was implying that she had fallen in love with him.

"Do you think you're in love with him?" he jeered.

"I haven't really known him long enough," attempting to protect herself from his biting cynicism.

"Surely love strikes like a lightning bolt?" he mocked, openly amused by her defensive attitude. The quelling look she gave him bounced off without leaving a mark. Subtly his manner changed, dropping the cold disdainful look to wrap her in the virile and disarming force of his maleness.

"Have you ever felt a man's caress?" Low laughter accompanied the rising color in her cheeks. "I thought not." The gleam in his gaze sent the blood racing to her face. A tanned hand touched a pink cheek, tingling her senses with the feather lightness of his touch. The tips of his fingers trailed down to her lips, brushing the sensual line of her lower lip. "I wonder what you'd look like if I made love to you?"

"Stop it!" Laurie demanded hoarsely, pushing his hand away in self-defense. She had already experienced his seductive ability when he had kissed her by the pool, and she had no doubt that he knew how to arouse a woman's desires. At this moment she could feel his irresitible magnetic pull.

"You didn't find my embrace so distasteful this afternoon," Rian reminded her complacently, a malicious dancing gleam in his dark eyes.

"You took me by surprise then," Laurie replied, fighting the odd breathlessness his nearness was causing.

"And now?" His mouth moved hypnotically closer.

"And now I don't want you to touch me," she answered quickly.

In the next instant her wrist was released and Rian was leaning back against his own cushioned seat, an amused chuckle shattering any impression that her weak words had halted him if he had wanted to kiss her.

"You don't have to worry," he taunted. "Seducing young girls in the back seat of a car is not my style. I've become accustomed to more adaptable surroundings and more experienced women."

Flames of hot embarrassment coursed through her body until Laurie felt suffused with color. "I hate you!" she rasped out in a voice trembling with anger and humiliation. "You're a despicable, arrogant beast! LaRaine is lucky to be rid of you."

"But you aren't so lucky." The slightly upturned corners of his mouth straightened into a grim forbidding line, reminding her that her insolence wouldn't go unpunished. "You're my fiancée."

"I'll never marry you!" she declared vehemently. "And you can't make me!"

"Don't be too sure about that." There was a proud flare of his nostrils that set off the dark aquiline features. "For the time being, I'll settle for your agreement to the engagement."

"Why should I?" Laurie demanded, tossing back her black hair to eye him coldly.

"Have you forgotten Vera?"

In the force of his baleful stare, the blue eyes blinked hesitantly. All thought of anyone else save the man sitting next to her had momentarily been wiped from her mind. Weakly Laurie knew she didn't want Vera to find out about the deception. She had grown fond of the woman, but to be truly Rian's fiancée was a price she had not bargained to pay to keep Vera's respect.

"You can't be getting cold feet?" Rian mocked. "After all, she's already convinced you're my fiancée, thanks to your masquerade."

"I won't marry you." Her voice was quiet, but it carried grim determination.

Rian smiled without amusement. "'Let the day's own trouble be sufficient unto the day.' We'll cross the other bridge when we come to it," he stated.

"That was. . . a quotation from the Bible," she announced with considerable surprise.

"You forgot," he jeered softly, "Satan was once an angel."

Had she just made a pact with a devil, Laurie wondered, studying the arrogantly carved jet black hair. The interior car light was switched off, plunging her into darkness. As the motor sprang to life, Laurie shivered and huddled more deeply into her seat. She had yielded to his overpowering presence, succumbed to the temptation of not having to tell Vera of her deception.

CHAPTER SIX

LAURIE SPENT A RESTLESS uncomfortable night.
Her troubled conscience kept sleep just out of
reach. Morning came all too soon with the grim
reminder that she was Rian's fiancée and Rian was
here in the same house with her. She tarried as long
as possible in her room before finally trekking
downstairs dressed in rust gold slacks and jacket.
Rian was standing near the front door talking to
Vera, an attaché case in his hand, as Laurie
reached the hallway.

"I was trying to persuade Rian to wait a few
more minutes," Vera called out gaily, "that you
were usually an early riser like me."

Ignoring Rian's speculating dark gaze, Laurie
kept her attention fixed on the smartly dressed
silver-haired woman. She knew his keen eyes
would pick up the pale shadows under her vivid
blue eyes and astutely guess that he was the cause
of her sleeplessness.

"You woke up in time to say goodbye to me,"
he declared sardonically as she halted next to Vera.

"Goodbye?" Laurie repeated with a frown of
disbelief, unwillingly glancing up at his aristocratic
face to make sure she had heard correctly.

"Yes," Vera grimaced ruefully beside her. "He barely arrives and he's dashing off on another business trip."

"I have a plane to catch," Rian informed Laurie. "You can walk me to the car."

"Have a safe journey," Vera wished before squeezing his hand in farewell and quietly retreating to leave Laurie and Rian alone.

His smile mocked her disconcerted expression as he opened the door and waited for Laurie to pass. His hand rested very lightly on her waist as she walked unresistingly toward the white Continental.

"Aren't you curious where I'm going?"

"No." A mutinous gleam in her clear blue eyes. "Only how long you'll be gone."

"Don't be sarcastic, Laurie love," he warned, his jaws hardening at her defiant expression. "I know you would like to see the back of me, but I didn't get you into this situation. It was of your own making."

"You were very quick to take advantage of it," she accused, flinching under the velvet whip of his false endearment.

"Do you blame me for protecting my family?" Rian asked. "That's what you claim you were doing."

"Not claim," she corrected sharply. "I was."

"I would advise you not to give in to any quixotic impulse and tell Vera the truth or attempt to run away. E.J. has been fully informed of the situation," Rian told her coldly, "and under my orders to take whatever action is necessary to prevent any movement you may try to make to alter things."

Laurie couldn't honestly admit that such thoughts had not crossed her mind, but she was too proud to tell Rian. "Don't you trust me to keep our bargain?" she demanded instead.

"I don't trust any woman, and least of all you."

"I don't trust you either."

Dark eyes glittered down at her as his mouth curved into a mocking smile. "How strange you should say that when I remember only a few nights ago hearing you say how you loved me and missed me terribly."

Laurie couldn't stop the swift rush of color to her face. "You know why I said that."

"And very convincingly done, too," he teased wickedly. "I think you're a much better actress than LaRaine."

Her eyes rounded enormously as she stared up at him. "Did you guess then that I wasn't LaRaine?"

"No." Straight brows gave him a hooded look. "The telephone call troubled me because I didn't expect Vera to exhibit such wholehearted affection for LaRaine. And you, as LaRaine, weren't very talkative, but it didn't occur to me that someone was impersonating her. Does that satisfy you?"

"Yes," Laurie replied quietly, not knowing whether it did or not.

Rian tossed the attaché case onto the passenger seat, then turned back to Laurie. "Vera is watching from the window. It's time for you to test your acting ability by kissing me a fond farewell.''

"I will not!"

With the lightning swiftness she was beginning to associate with him, Rian seized her chin in his hand, holding it up for her mouth to receive his kiss. His sweetly savage touch claimed her lips, lingered for a wildfire moment, then moved away so the glittering mockery of his dark eyes could laugh at her flashing blue glare. Her chin was still imprisoned by his lean fingers, but she raised a hand to wipe away the burning kiss from her mouth. Rian captured it, too, before it could accomplish its task.

"I wouldn't do that," he warned, a malicious light in his eyes as they danced over her outraged expression. "I would only have to replace that kiss with another...unless that's what you want me to do?"

He released her, openly challenging Laurie to try to defy him. Her hands dropped to her sides, clenched into useless fists of frustration.

Rian smiled complacently. "Now you're being sensible. Stay that way until I get back."

"How long will you be gone?" The question was drawn through clenched teeth.

His gaze narrowed for a moment. "A loving fiancée would want to know when I would be back."

"How long will you be gone?" she repeated, defiantly tilting her head.

"I'll see you tomorrow."

Her feet were implanted in the ground, incapable of carrying her away even when he crawled into the car and left. She stared after it, aware that she must look the picture of a dutiful fiancée savoring the last moments she had spent with her lover. But the fire that consumed Laurie was one of burning rage and loathing. Her generally placid nature had undergone a dramatic change, sparked by Rian's volatile and forceful personality. She had sworn last night to remain indifferent to him, to ignore his mocking jibes. The wildfire feeling that raced through her veins when she was with him disturbed her and Laurie shied away from attributing any cause other than that of her dislike for the man as the reason behind the unnerving sensation.

Still staring after the already vanished car, Laurie didn't hear the horses approach until the judge's stentorian voice broke into her reverie.

"Don't look so downhearted, Laurie."

She turned sharply, taking in the saddled horses he was leading.

He took note of the troubled frown on her face. "Don't tell me Rian has left you already?"

"Yes, a business trip," Laurie sighed as Vera walked out of the front door wearing her tan riding breeches and followed by Rian's bespectacled secretary, who was to be her watchdog.

"When will he be back?" the judge prompted with a cheery salute to the silvery fair woman coming toward them.

"Tomorrow."

"Then there's no reason to cancel our plans for this evening, is there, Vera?" he declared.

"No, I don't suppose there is," she agreed absently while Laurie caught the questioning look from E.J. Denton.

"What plans are those?" Rian's man inquired with an unassuming smile.

"Colin was escorting Laurie to an evening Mardi Gras parade after the four of us had dined," the judge explained. "When Rian arrived yesterday we had intended to cancel our plans, but there's no need to now that he's gone away again."

The hesitant look on E.J. Denton's face prompted Laurie to endorse the judge's idea. "Of course there's no need to change our plans," she declared with false heartiness, glad of the opportunity to thumb her nose at the absent Rian. "Colin has told me so much about the evening parades, and who knows when I'll be back here again during Mardi Gras time. Rian couldn't possible object." Rebellious sapphire eyes were turned on E.J., daring him to raise an objection.

"You're more than welcome to join us," Vera invited warmly.

E.J. Denton glanced at Laurie, realizing that she had been told he was to keep an eye on her. "No, thank you," he refused politely. "I have a great deal of paperwork to catch up on for Rian. This evening will be a perfect opportunity. You go ahead and enjoy yourselves."

"If that's settled, are you ladies ready for a

morning ride?'' The judge's twinkling gaze was directed lovingly at the smiling Vera.

''Laurie hasn't had time for breakfast yet,'' Vera hesitated.

''Fine. I had Mrs. Lawson prepare a brunch. We can ride directly to my place so Laurie can eat.''

''That sounds like a wonderful idea,'' Laurie declared with a laugh, wondering with wicked glee how poor E.J. Denton was going to keep an eye on her at that distance.

But the thought didn't trouble him as he lifted a hand in goodbye. ''Have a good time.'' Then he retreated toward the house, probably knowing that Rian's threat had been sufficient to keep Laurie in line. Recognizing her own weakness, Laurie had to admit he was right.

The day passed swiftly, too swiftly for Laurie, who felt like a bird freed from its cage. She felt she had to savor each moment of freedom before her master returned her to the cage. The fictitious master of her fate took the form of Rian. Even when his name wasn't mentioned in the conversation, he was uppermost in her thoughts. Some inner sense told her he would not be pleased to discover she was spending the evening with Colin. So, perversely, Laurie was doubly attentive to her bronzed escort.

The frenzied festivities of Mardi Gras complemented her high-strung gaiety. The laughing, shouting crowd that gathered along the parade route helped strip Laurie of her inhibitions as she joined in to add her voice to their joyful noise.

Dress was unimportant. A few people were dressed in outrageous costumes while others wore conventional sports clothes. Some, like Laurie and Colin, wore dressier attire. But the infectious high spirits made her lose all thought of the expensive silk dress of large black flowers against a background of white or the hand-crocheted shawl that covered her bare shoulders.

A self-propelled golden dragon weaved its way through the congested street, a hidden generator system providing the power to light all the myriad bulbs along its snaking back. A group of masquers, this time men in bright oriental dress and variegated masks covering their faces, was ensconced in a carrier on the dragon's back, tossing candy, toys, and costume jewelry to the delighted shrieks of the crowd. Laurie and Colin both raised their hands in a riotous effort to persuade the masquers to throw their booty in their direction.

Young and old alike scrambled for the tidbits tossed from the floats, playfully fighting over the inexpensive gifts and mementos as if they were pieces of eight. Equestrian units separated the floats and the marching bands. Elaborately dressed riders were astride beautiful prancing horses, their hooves gilded in silver or gold, with ribbons in their manes and false tails arching high over their backs.

There was a lull in the procession and Laurie happily reflected on the accuracy of Colin's earlier remark that Mardi Gras was a frivolous time when

Mobile went a little bit mad. Mardi Gras—Fat Tuesday, when every whim was indulged and reckless merriment ran rampant. Mardi Gras—followed by Ash Wednesday and the sobering fasting time of Lent.

"Oh, Colin, this is so much more fun than watching the parade from the window!" Laurie exclaimed, her face upturned so he received the full glow of her excitement.

"I haven't had this much fun at a parade since I was a child," Colin admitted laughingly.

"I've never had this much fun," Laurie declared fervently. "I feel like letting my hair down and going a little bit wild."

"Your hair is already down." A huskiness came into his voice as he captured a silken black lock in his hand. "And you're driving me a little bit mad. I feel like taking you into my arms and asking you where you've been all my life. Where have you been, Laurie?"

The ardent light in his hazel eyes sobered Laurie. After the possessively savage sweetness of Rian's mouth, she wondered what it would be like if Colin kissed her. Would he be tender and gentle as she had always wanted a lover to be? Or would he be demanding and sensual like Rian? Colin's hand moved from her hair to her shoulder as he saw the invitation written in the sparkling anticipation of her cerulean eyes.

The crowd surged around them, jostling their way forward as another float drew alongside. The moment when Laurie wanted the answer to her

tantalizing question passed and she eagerly turned
to the gaily festooned float, withdrawing the invitation and concentrating on the parade. Colin
was quick to sense the change. Although a flash of
regret passed across his eyes, he immediately
reverted to the carefree mood of those around
them.

With the passing of the float, the crowd eased
back to permit a marching band to pass. Laurie
rubbed the back of her neck, trying to rid herself
of the odd prickling sensation that was tingling
down her spine. A strong force compelled her to
glance over her shoulder, her eyes locked by the
tall man's where he leaned nonchalantly against a
tree.

With languid grace, Rian straightened and, still
holding her gaze, made his way through the crowd
to her side. He was wearing the dark business suit
from this morning, but his tie was loosened and
the buttons of his white shirt were undone to reveal
the tanned column of his throat.

"Rian! We didn't expect you back tonight!"
Colin exclaimed.

Laurie couldn't speak; her gaze was pinned by
the enigmatic expression on Rian's carved face.
"So I understand," he replied smoothly, his dark
eyes not leaving Laurie's upturned face.

Colin glanced hesitantly from one to the other,
in spite of Rian's reply feeling shut out by their
concentration in each other.

"I hope you don't mind my bringing Laurie to
the parade." An apologetic tone crept into his

voice. "She's never attended any Mardi Gras festivities before."

"You seemed to be enjoying yourself, Laurie," Rian commented.

"I was...I am," she quickly corrected herself, but not before there was a cynical lift to Rian's mouth.

"It's a pity I arrived to spoil your fun," he jeered softly. "I thought my fiancée might miss me."

"Colin and I are friends," she inserted hastily, not wanting Rian to put the wrong conjecture on their evening. The catch in her throat made her voice sound soft and breathless.

"In that case," for the first time Rian turned his gaze on Colin's uncomfortable expression, "you won't object if I take Laurie home."

"Of course not." The blond head nodded in agreement; Colin was fully aware, as Laurie was, that Rian expected no other answer.

Lines of fatigue were etched around the dark eyes. Laurie's natural concern for the well-being of others, regardless of her personal feelings, prompted her to suggest, "Would you like to leave now?"

"Would you excuse us?" Rian made a courteous nod in Colin's direction before slipping a guiding hand on Laurie's shoulders and moving her through the crowd before she had a chance to take back her suggestion. "I had to park several blocks away because of the congestion by the parade. I hope you don't object to walking," he remarked, releasing her once they were free of the milling people.

Laurie assured him that she didn't as they walked along the sidewalk of a tree-lined street.

"I suppose Mr. Denton told you where we were." Her voice sounded sharper than she had intended it to be, but his presence always set her nerves on edge.

"E.J. was under the impression it was to be a foursome. He was a bit upset when the judge and Vera returned to the house without you and Colin," said Rian, casting a downward glance at the defensive tilt of her chin. "The poor man thought there might have been a conspiracy to spirit you away."

"Is that why you came searching for us? Weren't you afraid you wouldn't find us in the crowd?"

"A native of the city becomes familiar with the best places to view a parade. I had a fair idea where Colin would take you," chasing away Laurie's theories with a dismissive shrug of his shoulders. "As for spotting you in a crowd, you haven't the type of face or figure that a man would overlook."

"Really?" Laurie retorted with chilling disbelief. "I doubt that you even knew I existed in Los Angeles."

"I can hardly be blamed for not being anxious to renew my acquaintance with LaRaine's cousin after our first meeting when you had that cream all over your face, your head swathed in a towel, and wearing a terribly unflattering red robe,'' Rian mocked. "The only thing worth looking at then was your blue eyes. The next time I saw you, you were much more presentable, but you seemed terribly anxious to fade into the wallpaper rather than attract my attention.'' Laurie could feel his dark gaze resting on her warm cheeks. "Why was that?''

"I didn't like you very much,'' she defended herself, while surprised to find out that he had noticed her.

"And you like me even less now.''

"That's true,'' she answered, hoping to destroy some of his complacency with her frankness.

"A little candor is refreshing, Laurie, but don't overdo it.'' His words acted as a gentle slap on the hand. "And you're playing with fire the way you keep leading Colin on.''

"I don't know what you're talking about.'' A betraying flush of color lent a falseness to her words as she wondered how long Rian had been standing there watching her and Colin.

"I've seen that look on a woman's face before which says she's curious to know what it would be like to be kissed by a certain man. I advise against any such experimenting,'' he told her firmly, a lingering of an unspoken threat in his voice.

The way he was presuming to dictate to her was irritating Laurie. She reared her head back like an unbroken filly bridling at her first touch of the bit. "You don't own me!'' she flared.

His fingers closed over her left wrist, holding up

her hand so the dim street light reflected the sheen of the deep blue sapphire and the flanking diamonds. "For the present, I do."

"You blackmailed me into wearing that ring." Her voice quivered with anger. "It doesn't mean any more to me than it did to LaRaine."

"I warned you not to push me," Rian snarled, whirling her around to face him while capturing her other wrist in his hand and twisting her arms behind her back. He forced her against the leanness of his hips and thighs, unmercifully bending her arms until pain shot through her shoulders. "Why did you do it?" His dark gaze rested on her downcast face, unable to struggle without incurring more pain from his steel hands. "Did you hope to make me angry enough to send you away? Or was it something else you wanted?"

"Let me go!" her order turning into a plea.

Rian chuckled coldly, tightening his grip enough so that Laurie's head tilted back to elude the knife-sharp pain. His mouth covered hers with demanding fierceness. Laurie tried to turn her head aside, but Rian ruthlessly wrenched her arms higher on her spine until she turned back to him. Her back was arched against the granite strength of his body and she could feel the thudding of his heart against hers. There was torturous madness in the burning kiss that melted away the pain of his hold. Her lips were being ground against her teeth as she unconsciously fought to keep from being drawn into the vortex of his anger. But Rian demanded submission. Yet when her lips ceased resisting his pressure, he still wasn't satisfied until they became pliant and responsive to his.

His virility had Laurie reeling as his touch became less forceful and more sensually persuasive. The light-headedness made her lose touch with reality. When his hold loosened on her wrists, she wasn't aware of it, although she knew the movements of his hands across her hips and back were setting off explosive charges that quaked through her body. At his insistence, her lips parted to allow his sensual exploration of her mouth. When Rian had her weakly clinging to him, achingly aware of her desire for him, he released her, holding her away so his dark eyes could glitter triumphantly down on her shaken face.

Instinctively Laurie swayed closer to him, the raging spell of his embrace still holding her captive. She could feel his black eyes dwelling on her lips, bruised by his passion and parted in an unwilling urgency to know again the soul-destroying fire of his kiss. Never before had she been so stirred by a man's touch or made so aware of the difference and delights of being a female in the arms of a male.

"You're very desirable," Rian murmured, his voice stroking her like a velvet glove. "I can see how you've managed to ensnare Colin with those innocent blue eyes. It's unfortunate for you that I'm not so easily fooled."

"What do you mean?" she breathed hoarsely, unwilling to believe the coldness that lay behind his softly caressing voice.

"First you blinked those big blue eyes at me, innocently pleading with me to understand. Then it was anger to persuade me to admire your spirit. When that didn't work, you became submissive and passionate. What will you try next in your attempt to lure me into letting you have your own way? Tears?" Rian taunted. "Such female tricks won't work on me, Laurie. I've long been immune to the wiles of a female. I can't be wrapped around your finger as Colin is. And I won't release you from our engagement that your pretense forced us into."

She refused to let the tears scorching the back of her eyes reveal themselves, knowing he would never believe they were there because of his arrogant accusation. Momentarily she had forgotten that he was used to a woman falling victim to his expertise in the art of love and his ability to shrug off the embrace that had brought such a shattering of her opinion that making love would be a warm and tender experience. For Laurie, it had been a volcanic eruption, tumultuous searing heat, that left her tossed about in the upheaval.

"You forced me to kiss you! I never asked for it nor invited it," she declared in a choked voice. "How dare you condemn me!"

"You'll find I'll dare a lot," he mocked, her indignant outburst amusing him. "But we did settle one question. You do belong to me."

"Never!" Laurie denied vigorously before her traitorous heart could declare otherwise.

Rian ignored her fervent avowal and placed a

hand on her rigidly erect back to guide her toward his car parked at the curb. His sureness that she was his to command made it clear how completely she had responded to his caress. But it was worse for Laurie to know that she wasn't as indifferent to him as she had thought. Like a magnet he attracted her, compelled her senses to acknowledge his masculinity, forced her to admit the desires of her flesh while his arrogance lashed out at her for being so weak.

The plush interior of the car was an exotic prison. She trembled at Rian's nearness even as her mind railed against it. Before he started the car, he tossed a sparkling object in her lap.

"Add this to the baubles you collected tonight," he ordered.

Despite the dim light, Laurie recognized the diamond and ruby-studded bracelet that had been Rian's first expensive gift to LaRaine. A stunned expression flashed across her face as she glanced at the chiseled profile behind the wheel.

"Where did you get this?" she whispered.

"LaRaine hurled it at me in a fit of pique."

"LaRaine?"

"I'm quite sure she regrets it now. It was an expensive bracelet."

"When did you see LaRaine?" unconsciously holding her breath as she waited for his answer.

"Today. She was nearly as stunned to see me as you were, but she recovered more quickly than you did." A laughingly cynical gleam was turned toward Laurie before Rian redirected his attention to the road.

"I thought you were away on a business trip."

"What business I conducted was secondary. The main purpose of the journey was to confront La-Raine."

"Was she very upset?" Laurie asked, picturing her cousin's reaction when she learned their masquerade had been uncovered.

"At first she was very contrite, almost convincingly humble, until she realized there would be no reconciliation—our relationship was truly finished. Her new acting career seems to have first place in her life now anyway, although she did become rather incensed when she learned that I was engaged to you."

"Why did you tell her that?" demanded Laurie.

"It's the truth. Why should I not tell her?" Rian mocked.

"It's a private arrangement for the benefit of your aunt, not an engagement in the true sense of the word."

"That's what you keep saying. Do you keep repeating yourself because you feel guilty that you've taken me away from LaRaine? As your cousin pointed out to me today, you're accustomed to picking up her leavings. Is a secondhand fiancé much different from a dress?" the cruel jibe biting into her pride.

"As far as I'm concerned I haven't got a fiancé, secondhand or otherwise," Laurie retorted coldly.

"Don't dismiss me so easily. You belong to me

for the time being." Hauteur iced his cutting tone.

The hard stones of the bracelet in her hand felt as unyielding as Rian. "Why did you give me this bracelet?"

"Why should you care? Avarice is a part of every woman's nature," he sneered cynically.

"No doubt that's the case with the women you've known," not caring how caustic her voice sounded as long as she could strike back with equal sarcasm. "They probably knew expensive presents were all you could give. Because a man with no heart is incapable of love."

"Damn your insolence!" Rian ground out with an arrogant flare of his nostrils as his dark eyes pierced the shadowy veil of her armor. The traffic around them was heavy which prevented him from stopping the car and raining his retribution on her. "Nobody talks to me that way!"

"It's time somebody did then." It was her turn to settle complacently in her seat.

But his hand seized her wrist, still bearing the marks from the last time. He drew her closer to him, his gaze not leaving the highway. "Why do you persist in riling my temper?" he demanded, uncaring of Laurie's gasps of pain. "Are you so uncertain of your ability to arouse a man's desire that you dare his wrath rather than his indifference?"

"No, that's not it at all." Her soft voice was made harsh by the fingers biting into the small bones of her wrist.

Rian spared a raking glance. "You're afraid of

me, aren't you? Hissing like a little kitten unable
to defend herself.''

"Yes, yes,'' she whispered, willing to agree with
anything that would prevent a further example of
his leashed violence and knowing there was a grain
of truth in his statement.

Her hand was released and Laurie sank back in
her seat massaging the soreness as Rian closed the
conversation. The silence of night was better than
the slinging barbs.

CHAPTER SEVEN

RIAN WAS NOT AT THE BREAKFAST TABLE the following morning, much to Laurie's relief. When she had passed the study, there had been voices and the sounds of shuffling papers. She had hoped that Rian was in there, but she didn't think her wish would be fulfilled until she had reached the dining area. The light repast of f grapefruit half, toast and coffee was quickly tucked away so Laurie could make her escape to the stables without enduring Rian's unsettling presence.

The cook-housekeeper had already informed her that Vera was there and the horses were saddled and waiting when Laurie arrived. A bemused smile crossed her face as she saw the judge hovering near the silver-haired woman. They looked so right together, he so tall and dignified and Vera so feminine and petite.

"Good morning, Laurie," the judge greeted her enthusiastically. "Did you enjoy the parade last night?"

"Yes, it was lovely. So colorful and unbelievably gay!" She flashed him a brilliant smile as she took the reins he handed her.

"Colin is on his way over. Here he comes now,"

he declared as he gave Vera a boost into her saddle and turned to look at the roan cantering toward them.

After a brief greeting that was lost in the impatient shuffling of the horses eager to be off, the four riders set out toward the beckoning countryside. As usual Colin and Laurie trailed behind the older couple, already engrossed in a private conversation.

"I never had an opportunity last night to tell you how much I enjoyed the parade," Laurie said after they had traveled some distance and the horses had become less frisky.

"I'm glad you did," Colin smiled, his warm gaze straying to the riders in front. "Last evening must have turned out well for the judge, too. He was singing this morning at the breakfast table. I haven't seen him that happy for ages. I'd have liked to have been a little mouse in the corner after we left them alone."

"They do act as if they're sharing some happy secret, don't they? I hope so. It would make all this seem worthwhile," Laurie mused wistfully.

"What do you mean—all this?" The blond Adonis immediately snapped up Laurie's slip of the tongue. "Don't tell me Rian was jealous about last night?"

There was a pause before Laurie answered as she felt her way for the words. "I hadn't told Rian of our plans for the evening, so he was a bit upset because he didn't expect me to be gone from the house when he returned."

"That explains it," Colin nodded. "For a minute there I thought Rian was going to come on as the heavy-handed fiancé posting No Trespassing signs on you. He can be very possessive toward anything he considers his."

Laurie blanched as she remembered the aggressive way Rian had said she belonged to him. She longed to deny her engagement with Rian, to prevent his brand from being stamped on her, while also remembering her own unqualified response to his embrace. She never dreamed it was possible to love and hate a man at the same time, flames of anger mixed with those of passion and desire.

"Not that I blame him," Colin added with a flirtatious twinkle in his gold-flecked eyes. "I wouldn't want anyone poaching on my reserves, if my reserves were you."

It was a statement made in jest, meant to lighten the dullness clouding her eyes. In answer, Laurie kicked her mount in the side, sending it off at a rapid canter while she tossed a laughing challenge at Colin. His roan bounded out immediately after her, its superior speed drawing them even in two strides. The pair swung out ahead of Vera and the judge, racing down the road to turn off into a meadow, then slowing their pace to a brisk trot.

"Say, what about the Mardi Gras Ball? Have you mentioned to Rian that I have tickets? I can easily get an extra one for him." Colin raised his voice slightly to carry over the blowing snorts of their horses.

"No, I haven't mentioned it. I'm not sure what

Rian's plans are." She didn't want to discuss Rian. Her feelings toward him were too complicated and there was too much simple beauty around them to ignore. Checking her mount down to a walk, Laurie breathed in deeply the fragrant country air. "I'm going to miss these early morning rides. They're such a perfect way to begin the day." As her shoulders made a regretful shrug, she knew also her departure would mark the end of her fraudulent engagement to Rian. The association with him had to be terminated as soon as possible before she was completely captivated by his animal attraction. "Only three more days."

Colin raised his light brown eyebrows in surprise. "Vera indicated that Rian would be staying at least another week. You aren't leaving before he does, are you?"

Another week! Laurie successfully concealed her astonishment at that statement as she silently wondered whether Rian was going to force her to stay until he left. There was a sickening lurch of her heart because she knew he would.

"I haven't decided," she replied, knowing the decision wasn't really hers to make now that Rian had installed himself as dictator. "Don't you think we should wait here for Vera and your father to join us?" she asked brightly, hoping to change the subject.

Their ride had taken them almost full circle back to the house. The dark shingles of the judge's roof could be seen through the treetops. Colin halted his horse and turned in the saddle.

"I thought Rian would be working this morning," he remarked casually.

Laurie whirled around, her gaze instantly picking out the dappled gray Arabian and the erect masculine figure astride the horse from the trio of riders approaching them. Her stomach contracted into a tight knot as she saw Rian separate himself from Vera and the judge, the Arab swinging out in an extended trot that had them gliding effortlessly over the gently undulating meadow.

A superb horse with a superb horseman on board, looking all the more imposing and ruggedly attractive in fawn-colored breeches and a white shirt, the jet black hair rakishly tousled by the teasing breeze. Laurie didn't stop staring even when Rian halted his spirited horse beside them.

"Good morning." Rian's greeting encompassed them both, but his sardonic gaze rested on Laurie's flushed face, coloring when she realized how rudely she had been staring.

"I didn't know you were going riding with us this morning," she murmured, feeling the need to say something. "I heard you in the study working when I came downstairs."

"That must have been E.J.," he shrugged, his hooded gaze leaving her at last to dwell on the tossing head of his horse. "Sitar and I were out watching the sunrise while you were still playing Sleeping Beauty. I considered going in and kissing you awake, but the temptation to join you under the bedcovers might have been too great."

"Rian!" Embarrassed anger tore his name from

her throat as Laurie glanced at the disconcerted expression on Colin's face.

"I think this is a private conversation," Colin remarked, touching a finger to his tanned forehead before reining his horse away to join the judge and Vera.

"You said that deliberately so he would leave." Laurie turned an accusing glance on Rian.

"Yes." Arrogance and mockery shone out of his aquiline face. "Which doesn't mean that the thought didn't occur to me to do exactly what I said."

"I might have had something to say about it," she retorted grimly.

"You might have... for a while." His dark eyes boldly took in the quick rise and fall of her breasts which revealed her inner agitation. A scarlet stain crept into her cheeks.

"You're egotistical and crude!" she spat.

Her angry accusation drew a chuckle from Rian. "Go ahead and lash out at me," he mocked. "But you know you always end up purring when I touch you."

The sensually intimate look in the burning black coals of his gaze momentarily robbed Laurie of her ability to breathe. Silently she acknowledged the physical attraction that drew her to him, likening herself to the moth drawn by the flame and hoping she would escape with no more than singed wings.

"That isn't enough," she declared angrily.

"In this enlightened age of sex, don't tell me

I've become engaged to a prim and proper Victorian miss,'' Rian jeered with considerable amusement.

"Hardly Victorian." Laurie didn't attempt to deny the rest of his description, knowing she was something of a prude when it came to the so-called "free love." "I won't be told by anyone who I'm to marry."

"Ah, yes," he nodded, stilling the prancing horse with the touch of his hand, "you're going to be in love with the man you marry, aren't you? What was it you said—he'll be tender and kind like Colin. Is that why the two of you had separated yourselves from the judge and Vera, so you could compare mutual likes and dislikes and discover whether you were compatible?"

"No, that isn't why Colin and I were off by ourselves," she declared, barely suppressing her rising temper. "If you must know, we were giving Vera and the judge a chance to be alone. That's also the reason we went to the parade without them."

"A pair of innocent matchmakers," Rian drawled sarcastically.

"Twist it any way you want to." Flashing him an angry glance, she moved her mount toward the slow-walking horses and riders.

The pushing shoulder of Rian's gray forced her to fall in behind the others instead of drawing level with them as Laurie had planned. There was a deep-seated desire to put a quirt to her horse's flank and race away, but she knew Rian's horse was faster than Briar and he would catch up with her in minutes.

Vera turned slightly in her saddle so she could see Rian and Laurie. "The judge has suggested that we have a party this Saturday to celebrate your engagement, a small affair with only our closest friends invited. But Colin reminded us that Laurie is leaving on Wednesday."

"Those plans were made before she knew I would be coming to Mobile," Rian replied, a bland expression on his lean features at the angry glance Laurie darted at him.

"You know I have other commitments in Los Angeles." The saccharine smile on her lips belied the honey-coated tone.

"They can be postponed a few days," he stated with his familiar autocratic manner, challenging her to disagree with his edict.

Laurie was so angry that he was deliberately prolonging her stay and thus prolonging their phony engagement that she would dare anything, especially when she knew his jeering tongue couldn't lash out at her in front of his aunt.

"You say that, darling," Laurie murmured loud enough for the others to hear as she put extra emphasis on the endearment, "because you have no idea all the things a bride has to do to prepare for the wedding."

"Such as?" One corner of his mouth twitched in amusement, laughing at the kitten trying to best the superior jungle cat.

"There are the bridesmaids to be chosen, the

wedding colors, the dresses, the wedding gown, the place for the reception, the guest list, the printed invitations, bridal showers, all that sort of thing," Laurie replied brightly.

"What will your colors be?" Womanly sharing of the excitement of the wedding that Vera couldn't know would never take place.

"Blue and black," Rian answered before Laurie could reply.

"What, black for her hair and blue for her eyes?" the judge inserted with a low chuckle. "They're a startlingly beautiful combination on Laurie, but hardly suitable for a bridal party, Rian."

"No, those are the colors Laurie will be if she thinks she's going to drag me through that kind of a ritualistic ceremony." The wicked gleam in his dark eyes was clearly visible to everyone.

"Have you set the wedding date?" Colin inquired.

"No. . ." Laurie began, only to have Rian interrupt her.

"Yes, in two weeks. We're going to elope." The certainty in his voice caught her off guard.

"We are not!" Laurie exclaimed, the denial that she was ever going to marry him springing instantaneously to her lips. "I told you. . . ."

Her words were broken off by the steel fingers biting into her arm and the hardness of his leg brushing against hers. "Watch it," he hissed for her ears alone, the glittering fire in his eyes as effective as his grip on her arm. As his gaze locked onto hers, there was a traitorous weakness flowing through her body, sapping her anger while increasing the beat of her heart.

"We aren't going to elope," Laurie finished in a quieter voice.

"You can't blame the girl, Rian, for wanting a big wedding with all the trimmings," the judge put in. "Every young girl pictures herself walking down the chuch aisle in a white satin gown."

"Do you picture yourself that way?" Rian baited quietly. "Walking down the aisle to me?"

Laurie couldn't answer. The image he painted in her mind's eyes stole her voice. She could visualize it completely, even to Rian's dark eyes compelling the steps she took toward him. She could almost hear his low voice making the the vows that united them. The mysterious light in his eyes closed out all thought of anyone beside the two of them.

"Has the cat got your tongue?" Rian whispered, releasing her arm and touching a finger to the softness of her lips.

Her heart skipped a beat as her lashes fluttered down over her blue eyes, concealing the flaming desire that his intimate caress sparked.

"You don't play fair, Rian Montgomery," she accused in a tight voice.

"I always get what I want, though," he replied with the twisted smile that didn't reach the glittering triumph in his eyes.

"Are you two lovebirds going to join us for brunch?" the judge broke in.

Laurie was startled to see the path leading to the

judge's rear patio. She hadn't realized they had come so far so quickly. She felt a trembling of relief to know that in a few minutes they would all be occupied with cool drinks and sandwiches, thus eliminating the possibility of more of Rian's private asides to her.

"Laurie and I will pass this time, judge," Rian drawled, turning his horse and thus forcing Laurie's horse to turn in the direction of home as well. "We'll catch a bite at the house with E.J."

By the knowing smiles that were exchanged between Vera and the judge, Laurie knew they were putting the wrong conjecture on Rian's words. They were obviously thinking that the two of them wanted to be alone, and that was the wish farthest from her mind.

"I'll see you later," Vera waved.

Large oaks, partially draped with Spanish moss, soon separated Laurie and Rian completely from the others as they walked their horses along the worn path to Vera's stables. Her tight-lipped silence didn't go unnoticed by Rian.

"What's arching your back this time?" he taunted, checking his Arab as it tried to hurry its pace.

"My back isn't arched," Laurie answered, unconsciously relaxing the rigidity of her position, which drew an amused chuckle from Rian.

"I declined the invitation, because I thought it was what you wanted."

"Why should I want to be alone with you?" Her cheeks colored as she made the angry retort.

"Perhaps I misunderstood." His calmness in-
furiated her. "I thought you wanted the judge and
Vera to be alone."

His answer flustered her. "I did. . . I do."

"But not if it means being alone with me, is that
it?"

"I didn't say that."

"You didn't have to," he replied.

Fluidly Rian dismounted at the paddock gate,
reaching out to hold the bridle of Laurie's chestnut
as she too slipped off her horse. His attention had
thankfully shifted from her to the horses.

"They're still a bit warm," he said, shoving the
chestnut's reins into her unwilling hands. "Let's
walk them out."

It was difficult walking beside Rian without being aware of him. The top of her tousled black hair
was even with his chin. A white shirt accented
rather than concealed the rippling leanness of his
muscular figure while the fawn breeches and
brown riding boots suited his rugged looks more
than the elegant suits had done. Rian Montgomery
was a man of action—arrogant and autocratic,
sure of his own power to control the lives of
others.

Living with him, Laurie thought idly, would be
like living on the side of a volcano. At times the
solid foundation would be comforting, but when
the rumblings began it would be terrifying.

She mustn't think like that, she told herself
firmly, discovering she was almost accepting his
presence as a permanent thing. It was the silence

dominated by the compelling man walking beside her that was inducing these introspective ramblings. Three more days and she would be gone. All of this would seem like a dream that had never really happened. Then Laurie remembered Vera mentioning the party.

"What about the party this weekend?" she asked hesitantly, unable to lift her gaze from the trodden sandy soil at her feet. "My plane reservations, or rather LaRaine's plane reservations, are for this Wednesday."

"They can be changed," his mocking voice reminded her.

"I know, but...you don't really want to have Vera give an engagement party for us."

"How do you know what I want?" A knife-sharp edge to his mockery.

Laurie didn't want to delve into that subject and subsided into silence.

"What prompted your sudden interest in the marital status of my aunt?" Rian asked, changing the subject with lightning swiftness.

Laurie blinked up at him briefly. "The first time I met the judge I knew he was quite taken with Vera. Later Colin mentioned that his father had been in love with her for years." She didn't want to mention that Colin had also told her of Rian's part in the breakup of Vera's previous marriage. "I thought it would be a wonderful thing if they finally got together."

"Wasn't one disastrous marriage enough for Vera?" Rian lashed out bitterly.

"Why...why would a marriage between the judge and Vera be disastrous? He loves her very much."

"Love! Love!" he ground out angrily. "You keep harping back to the same thing."

"What's wrong with love? It wouldn't be a marriage without it." Confusion darkened her blue eyes.

"Love destroys. It turns a man into a whipped dog and a woman into a dispirited slave," Rian bit out savagely.

"That's not true," Laurie gasped.

"Do you know any couple who are truly in love, the way you mean it? Aren't they together to satisfy mutual needs—food, lodging, clothing, companionship, and the physical gratification of the opposite sex?" he jeered.

Laurie knew so few people and none well enough to speak with authority on their personal lives. Her failure to answer brought more derogatory remarks from Rian.

"What about LaRaine's parents? A more greedy, selfish woman I've never met than Carrie Evans. It's no wonder your uncle spends all his waking hours at work!"

"But the judge," she protested weakly, not a match for his suddenly vicious attack, "look at how long he's loved Vera."

"Yes, and that same love destroyed his marriage. Jealousy ate away Colin's mother until she didn't care to live anymore. I know Colin must have told you what kind of a marriage Vera had,"

Rian said sarcastically. "All she ever meant to her husband was a ready income that didn't require work. He didn't even have to maintain a pretense of a happy marriage to fool Vera. She was so besotted with him, he made her the laughingstock of the city." Laurie was mesmerized by the anger and contempt in Rian's face. "I want no part of love!"

A twisting wrenching pain tore into her heart, making breathing almost impossible. She couldn't believe she was hearing correctly.

"What about your parents?" she asked.

"I saw my father nearly destroy his business trying to buy my mother's love with presents. He was an important man, a powerful man, but she drove him to his knees until he destroyed them both in a car crash." His mouth was a grim tight line, making him look more cruel and ruthless than Laurie thought possible. She couldn't meet the cold glitter of his gaze.

"Then why, why do you want to get married?" Her dark head moved from side to side as if to shake away the agony his words were creating.

"I told you once," Rian spoke derisively. "A woman has more uses than just to take to bed. I need a hostess, a housekeeper, and someone to bear my children."

"What about what your wife wants?" Her voice barely squeezed through the hard knot in her throat.

"She'll lack for nothing. You forget, I'm very wealthy."

"I was right about you." Tears were spilling over Laurie's pale cheeks. "You don't have a heart," she gulped, fighting to get the ring off her finger.

But Rian ripped her hand away, carrying it to his chest where he rested it against his thudding heart. "Yes, I do," he stated harshly, sweeping an arm about her waist and drawing her to the firmness of his body. "A woman doesn't want a husband, she wants a lover."

His mouth ground against hers, the salty taste of her tears moistening her lips to mingle with his. His primitive kiss transmitted his desires to her, sparking an answering flame that consumed all resistance to his touch. When Laurie was clinging to him, her fingers curled around his neck and into the ebony blackness of his hair. Rian lifted his head, breaking off the passionate embrace.

"Damn, but I want you, Laurie!"

"No!" The ragged denial was torn from her heart.

With a strength she didn't know she was capable of, Laurie twisted free. One backward step, then she was pivoting and racing toward the house while she still had some strength to resist his overpowering attraction.

CHAPTER EIGHT

A WIDE TREE-LINED PLAZA marked the end of the four-mile-long bridge that joined Dauphin Island to the mainland. The road was divided by lush green grasses dotted with spiky palmettos. Not a fleecy white cloud marred the azure blue heavens, and the glare of the golden sun was pleasantly warm. Laurie dutifully studied the scenery, determinedly keeping her gaze averted from the dark compelling man behind the wheel of the luxury car.

"Rian," Vera spoke up from her place in the back seat with the judge, "would you take Gerry and me to the harbor? He wants to check on his boat and I'm sure you would much rather show Laurie around the island yourself."

"I didn't know you had a boat, judge," Rian commented, ignoring his aunt's reference to Laurie.

"A very unostentatious cabin cruiser, just big enough for me to go out in the Gulf to do some deep-sea fishing," he replied. "I haven't been out since late fall. I thought I'd better make sure everything is all right there. You can pick Vera and me up later to picnic down by the beach."

"Would you feel safe in my company for a few

hours, Laurie?'' Lazy, half-closed black eyes glinted at her, the mockery in his drawling voice laughing at her rigidly controlled expression. Since their disastrous conversation yesterday morning, Laurie had taken pains to keep from being alone with Rian as his callous denunciations of love still ringing in her ears had caused a dull ache in her chest.

"What a silly thing to ask!" Vera exclaimed with a curious laugh. "She's your fiancée."

"But extraordinarily reluctant to endorse your suggestion." His statement forced Laurie to reply. She had hoped this excursion would remain a foursome and knew that Rian realized it too.

"On the contrary," the lightness in her voice was slightly brittle, "I think it should be very interesting to have you as my tour guide, Rian. You have such a unique point of view about things."

The subtlety of her comment was not lost on him as he acknowledged the point in her favor with a tilting nod of his dark patrician head.

After they had dropped Vera and the judge at one of the docks, Rian drove slowly along the marina area so Laurie could see the different boats tied up there. Sailing sloops bobbed beside inboard cabin cruisers, while farther down were the fishing boats.

"Every year there's a blessing of the fishing fleet," Rian told her. "The shrimp boats all wear their best nautical decorations. You see," he tossed her a mocking glance, "I take my duties as tour guide seriously." Not for anything would Laurie admit that his tidbit of information interested her, maintaining the silence of one waiting to be amused. "The next stop in our excursion is Fort Gaines."

"How familiar are you with the history of this area?" Rian asked when they walked into the inner courtyard of the fort.

"I hardly know anything about it," Laurie admitted, expecting a scornful glance, but she was met by a smile.

"Then let me be the first to enlighten you," tucking her hand under his arm and walking toward the ramp leading to the top of the fort wall. "Isle Dauphine, as the French called it when their first military expedition settled here in 1699, was an important base before the founding of the Louisiana Territory, which eventually stretched from the Gulf of Mexico to the Great Lakes and westward. The city of Mobile was the provincial capital of this French territory and Dauphin Island was the port of entry for two-thirds of the North American continent."

"I've always connected New Orleans with the Louisiana Territory," Laurie murmured.

"So do most people," Rian nodded. "Have you heard of the so-called 'cassette' girls of New Orleans?" Laurie shook her head that she hadn't. "Twenty-four years before they arrived in New Orleans, the French ship *Pelican* dropped anchor at Dauphin Island. On board were twenty-four young girls who were sent by the King of France to marry the men living here and persuade them to settle down near the fort on Mobile River, which was later the city of Mobile. They became known as the 'Pelican girls,' arriving in the colony almost a quarter of a century before their New Orleans counterparts.''

"Did they marry the men?"

"Naturally, they were here to serve their King." There was a slight pause during which Laurie could feel his dark gaze resting on her. "What? No outcry about loveless marriages?" he jeered. "Or is the notion of traveling across half the world to marry a total stranger romantic enough by itself?"

Her dark brows arched over cool blue eyes. ''I don't believe I'm required to answer questions put to me by an insolent tour guide.''

A humorless smile was directed at her. "Why am I insolent? Because I've asked you to be my 'Pelican girl'?"

"You never 'ask,' Rian. You order," Laurie sighed, knowing how easily he could intimidate her.

"Do you want me to ask?" his velvet-soft voice whispered near her hair as she stopped to look out of the southeast bastion.

"Rian, please!" His hand was on the silkiness of her long hair, slipping underneath to caress the sensitive cord along her neck.

"I like the way you say my name," came his husky declaration. "Say it again."

"No!" taking a quick step forward to elude his unnerving touch. The gulf water shimmered a blue green, almost turquoise color near the shore of white sand. "What's that out in the water?"

Laurie pointed, seeking to draw his attention away from her.

"That's the lighthouse on Sand Island marking the mouth of Mobile Bay," Rian replied, a tinge of cynical amusement in his voice. "There's been a lighthouse there since 1838 to guide the ships to a safe anchorage. This side of the lighthouse and beyond is where the famous Battle of Mobile Bay took place during the war between the States. Admiral Farragut commanded the fleet of four Union ironclad monitors while eighteen wooden Confederate warships formed a battle line protecting the entrance. It was here that Farragut made his famous remark 'Damn the torpedoes, full speed ahead!' The ironclads won and Mobile fell to the North." His hands settled on her shoulders, pulling her back against the hardness of his chest. "Haven't you ever wanted to say that? 'Damn the torpedoes, full speed ahead!' "

For a moment, Laurie relaxed against him, glorying in the masculine nearness that swept her breath away, inhaling the scent of his maleness, totally intoxicated by his overpowering virility. In that one split second, she wanted to say, "Damn love" and give herself up to his capable hands. But the weakness didn't last as she swallowed back her desire for his touch.

"Perhaps if I were guaranteed the victory, I might," she answered calmly, relieved when Rian's hands dropped to his side. Her ships were wooden and it was Rian who commanded the ironclads. If there was ever a battle, the victory would be his.

They continued along the path to the east bastion where Rian pointed out the companion Fort Morgan guarding the other side of the Bay, then walked on to the preserved northwest bastion complete with the vaulted ceilings and arches.

"The bricks used to construct the fort were shaped by slave labor," Rian explained. "The work was done near Dog River on the mainland almost twenty miles away. All these bastions had dual roles. They served as cannon ports, but the entire roof areas of each were catch basins for rainwater which was strained through a bed of shells and sand and carried to large cisterns beneath the floor of the fort and the yard."

"Was the fort ever used during the world wars?" Laurie inquired, preferring to keep to the safer topic of history.

"Yes, although it never saw battle action. A small garrison was stationed here in World War II, mostly to watch for saboteurs being landed here by enemy submarines which were frequently sighted off the mouth of Mobile Bay."

With their tour of the fort completed, Laurie and Rian viewed the artifacts on display at the Confederate Museum on the grounds before returning to the car. From the car windows, Laurie was shown the island's country club with the lush greens of an eighteen-hole golf course, the white beaches edged by the blue gulf water, and the large oak trees in Cadillac Square, named after one of the three French governors who lived on the island. As they retraced part of their route to the marina, Rian pointed out the oak trees growing on top of large mounds of empty oyster shells, mute testimony to the Indian tribes that lived here long before the first French explorer set foot on Isle Dauphine.

When the foursome was complete again, the talkativeness of Vera and the judge made up for the lack of conversation between Laurie and Rian. The laughter and happy voices of the older couple made Laurie feel that she and Rian were chaperoning them. The stretch of beach that Vera selected as the site for their picnic was empty except for the gulls that danced at the water's edge or flew screeching above the gentle waves.

It was an idyllic setting—a bright blue picnic blanket on white sugar sand, the salty tang of a gulf breeze, and the calming sound of the surf rushing in to kiss the shore. But Laurie couldn't relax. The expertly prepared seafood salad was tasteless to her. She was almost glad when everyone was finished and the food was packed away in the hamper again.

For all the notice Rian paid her she might as well not have been there. An hour before he had been all charm, undermining her defenses and twisting her into knots. Laurie had been telling herself that she didn't want him to pay attention to her, to touch her, to cast his spell on her. Now that he was doing none of these things, she perversely wanted him to.

"How about a stroll along the beach, Laurie?" Rian was on his feet, looking down at her with a mocking glint in his eyes.

A second ago she had craved his attention, but with his invitation hanging in the air, Laurie hesitated to accept. Any time spent alone with Rian Montgomery was dangerous to her peace of mind. A brown hand stretched out to take hold of hers and she found herself placing her hand in it as he helped her to her feet without a word of agreement being spoken.

"I believe they would prefer to be alone," Rian commented with a half smile after he and Laurie had walked several yards.

"I thought you didn't approve of. . . Vera and the judge?" Confusion marred the clearness of her eyes.

"Vera is old enough to make her own mistakes. I wouldn't consider interfering," he replied indifferently before casting her a mocking glance. "Besides, there's probably something to be said for companionship in your old age. I should have listed that as one of the considerations for marriage."

"You certainly aren't old." Her cheeks were flushing for no apparent reason.

"I'm older than you by several years."

"So is Colin." The instant Laurie said that, she wanted to take it back. She had meant to show her indifference to age and not to wave a red flag to start another argument between her and Rian. "I'm sorry," she apologized quickly, not daring to meet his eyes. "I only meant that someone is bound to be older than someone else."

There was a moment of silence before Rian replied, "I accept your apology."

An indefinable truce had been declared. The snow white beach stretched out as endlessly as the sea on the horizon and Laurie felt she could walk forever. There was no need for conversation. There was only the insatiable thirst to drink in the magic of these moments walking side by side with Rian, knowing his strides were shortened to match companionably with hers. They didn't touch, not even their hands, but Laurie felt closer to him than she ever had before. They were as one with the earth and sky and sea.

"We've lost sight of Vera and the judge," Laurie murmured, unwilling to break the silence, yet not being able to believe that Rian was content as she.

"We wouldn't make very good beachcombers." Rian's steps had slowed to a halt as he turned a whimsical smile toward her. "We can't lose touch with reality and keep going."

"Think how bored you would become with the monotony of a beachcomber's life," she remarked idly, tilting her head sideways to study his bland expression. "You enjoy the challenge of the business world, organizing companies and watching them grow."

A sudden puff of wind from the gulf whipped her blue black hair across her face. Before her own hand could brush it back, Rian's was there gently lifting it from her face and tucking it behind her ear, then leaving his hand to cup her cheek.

"I've never found the company of a tantalizing female to be soothing before now." The velvet softness of his voice reached out to stroke her already purring heart.

"Rian." His name was a husky sound born in her aching need for his warmth. For an instant his hand tightened, promising to erase the space that separated them, then a rueful smile tilted a corner of his mouth, followed by a little sigh.

"We must go back," he said firmly, dropping his hand from her cheek and leaving her with a cold feeling that wouldn't go away even when the sun touched it.

"Yes," Laurie breathed in reluctant agreement before chiding herself for that reluctance. It was just as well that she was removed from his compelling influence. Too much time spent in his company was a dangerous thing.

The walk back took too little time. So did the drive to Vera's house. Almost the instant they set foot in the door, Rian excused himself, saying he had work to do. Laurie watched him striding toward the study, a sense of loss stealing over her.

Almost an hour later Laurie saw Rian from her bedroom window as he crawled into the white Continental and left. Restlessly, she prowled her room, eventually wandering downstairs in search of Vera, only to find she had gone over to the Hartford house. The blue of the swimming pool gleamed invitingly in the late afternoon sun, but Laurie wasn't in the mood. Finally she settled in one of the emerald green sofas in the living room and leafed through a magazine. The telephone jingled on a nearby stand. Laurie waited, expecting

E.J. to pick up the extension in the study, but the telephone kept ringing. Hesitantly Laurie picked up the receiver.

"Is Rian Montgomery there?" a woman's voice asked.

"Not right now," Laurie replied. "He should be back later. May I ask him to call back?"

"Is that his aunt?"

"No, this is Laurie Evans." Reluctant to voice her tenuous relationship to Rian.

"Are you Rian's fiancée? He mentioned that you were staying with Vera."

The woman's swift recognition of her surprised Laurie. Her acknowledging "yes" was hesitant as she wondered who the melodic voice belonged to on the other end of the line and how the woman was associated with Rian.

"I'm so glad I have this chance to talk to you!" the woman exclaimed. "You're a very lucky girl to have someone like Rian."

"Yes, thank you," Laurie stumbled, finding any other reply unsuitable.

"How silly of me! I haven't even introduced myself," the woman laughed. "I'm Liz Trevors. My husband Arnold works for Rian. Or at least, he was working for him. That's what I was calling to tell Rian—that the doctors have said he can go back to work in a month. They're releasing him from hospital tomorrow."

"I'm glad to hear that," Laurie replied, wondering if LaRaine had known the Trevors, hence if she should.

"I doubt that Rian mentioned it to you. He isn't one to bring his work home. My husband was injured in an automobile accident some three months ago and has been hospitalized ever since. Rian has been our guardian angel, making sure I had transportation to and from the hospital, seeing to it that the children were looked after, taking care of the hospital bills. And he's been a tremendous boost to my husband's morale by keeping Arnold up to date with the company's transactions and assuring him that the position would be open whenever Arnold was able to come back. That's not even mentioning the fact that Rian kept him on the payroll all the while he was in the hospital. Every time we try to thank him, Rian just shrugs it off. I'm so glad I'm able to tell you how grateful we are for all your fiancé has done."

The picture Mrs. Trevor painted of Rian as a thoughtful and considerate employer didn't match Laurie's image of a domineering and ruthless man whose charm was laced with cruelty and a desire to gain his own ends.

She was still mulling over this discovery when she replaced the receiver and heard E.J. walk in the front door. He waved a greeting to her as he walked past the arched doorway.

"A Mrs. Trevors just called for Rian," Laurie told him, walking into the hallway to follow E.J.

"Arnold Trevors' wife?" he asked, adjusting the black-rimmed glasses on his nose.

"Yes, she wanted to let Rian know that her husband is being released from the hospital tomorrow and should be back to work in a month.''

"That's a relief,'' raising his eyebrows in an expressive gesture. "Heaven knows, Rian and I couldn't keep doing the work of a third person for much longer.''

"Does Mr. Trevors have an important position?'' Laurie asked curiously.

"He was handling the South American deal until the accident, when Rian had to take over. That was about the time Rian met LaRaine.'' As soon as Laurie's cousin's name was out of his mouth, E.J. cast her an apologetic look.

"Yes, well....'' Laurie breathed in deeply, not wanting to go into any details regarding the abrupt change brought on by her masquerade as LaRaine, so she sought the quickest excuse to end the conversation. "You will pass Mrs. Trevors' message on to Rian when he returns, won't you?''

"Of course.''

Rian didn't return for the evening meal and Vera and Laurie ate alone while E.J. had sandwiches served for himself in the study. Not until nearly ten o'clock when Laurie was mounting the stairs to her room did Rian return. He glanced briefly at his watch and bade her an absent goodnight before continuing on to the study where E.J. was still working.

Laurie turned and tossed in her bed, dozing off, then awakening, unconsciously listening for the sound of Rian's footsteps in the hall. After awakening from another fitful doze, she glanced at the jeweled clock on the night stand. The luminous dial illuminated the time as three o'clock. Rising from the bed, she slipped on her ivory satin dressing robe and walked quietly into the hallway, deciding that a glass of warm milk might chase away her sleeplessness.

At the bottom of the stairs she could see a light shining from the study door. Rian couldn't possibly be working this late, Laurie thought idly as she tiptoed toward the door. But when she glanced in, she saw Rian sitting behind the desk, his suit coat tossed over a chair with his tie, and his white shirt unbuttoned at the throat. He was wearily rubbing his hand across his forehead while holding the telephone receiver to his ear. Some infinitesimal sound betrayed her presence and caused him to glance up.

He cupped a hand over the receiver. "What are you doing up?"

"I couldn't sleep," Laurie answered softly, clutching the robe tighter around her throat. "I was going to get some warm milk."

"Make it cocoa and I'll have a cup," Rian ordered, taking his hand from the receiver to speak into it while Laurie retreated quietly toward the kitchen.

Rian was no longer on the telephone when Laurie came back carrying two steaming mugs of cocoa on a small circular serving tray. Raking his fingers through the blackness of his hair, he rose from the desk chair.

"Set it down over by the sofa," he instructed.

Obediently Laurie walked to the brown leather

sofa and placed the tray on the oak coffee table in front of it. Uncertain whether she was to stay or go, she remained standing, removing her mug from the tray. Rian sank down into the leathery cushions, glancing up at her erect figure in surprise that soon turned to bemusement.

"Don't stand there like a rabbit about to take flight. Sit down and keep me company."

She chose a large armchair in matching brown leather, folding her fingers around the warm cup to still their trembling. Rian looked so tired, leaning forward as though to relax against the back of the sofa would bring instant sleep.

"Do you have to work so late?" she murmured.

"Late?" One corner of his mouth tilted in a humorless smile. "It may be three o'clock here, but it's nine o'clock in the morning in London."

"Is that where you were calling?" Laurie asked, watching the lean hands as they lifted the mug to his mouth.

"Mmmm, yes," he replied, replacing the cup on the tray to press his fingers against the center of his forehead.

"Do you have a headache?"

"Tension more than anything," Rian shrugged.

Laurie hesitated, longing to offer to massage his neck and ease those lines of fatigue around his eyes and mouth but afraid he would misconstrue her interest. Finally she gathered the courage.

"Would you like me to rub your neck?" she asked.

A dark eyebrow arched at her with mocking inquiry before Rian obligingly moved toward the end of the sofa, stretching his long legs out on the cushioned seat. Her hands trembled as she tentatively touched the taut cords of his neck. Then gently she began massaging the skin, enjoying the sensation of unrestricted touch. As her nervousness went away and her touch became more firm, she felt Rian relaxing, the stiffness leaving his neck. When her hands moved to his temples, he moved slightly in surprise, then settled deeper in the cushions to rest his head against the arm of the sofa. The lids were closed over his dark eyes so he couldn't see her studying the harsh lines of his face and watching them soften.

Her fingers were beginning to ache when she noticed his even breathing and knew Rian had fallen asleep. Laurie smiled down at him, thinking how much younger and gentler he seemed. Very quietly she moved to the far end of the room where a gold and brown afghan lay folded on a table. For a moment Laurie held it against her breast, staring down on the masculine form lying on the couch. A warm glow spread happily through her, filling her with a burning tenderness as she realized she had fallen in love with Rian Montgomery. Perceptively she knew she had been in love with him for a long time, but had refused to admit it.

A tiny sigh broke from her lips. It was a futile love, one that Rian didn't return, although admittedly he wanted her in a carnal way. So as the acknowledgement of her love for Rian stole over her, a bitter taste mingled with the sweet.

Unfolding the afghan, Laurie gently draped it over Rian's still form, wishing she could curl up in his arms and nestle her head against his chest. As she reached out to bring the coverlet over his white shirt, she saw his eyelids flutter open.

"Are you tucking me in for the night?" he asked lazily.

Laurie caught her breath, knowing how vulnerable she was at that moment with the blackness of his eyes studying the pink in her cheeks. If Rian should learn of her love for him, it would give him unlimited power over her. She hadn't decided yet whether she wanted to marry a man who didn't love her even though she was deeply in love with him.

"Yes," she answered briskly, lowering her gaze so he couldn't read her thoughts as he usually did.

His hand closed lightly over her wrist. "Are you going to kiss me good-night, too?"

Laurie knew that if she didn't take the initiative in complying to his mocking question, Rian was quite capable of forcing her to kiss him. Bending over, she lightly brushed his lips with hers and moved away.

Rian chuckled softly and released her wrist. "If I weren't so tired, I'd make you do better than that." A crooked smile curved his mouth as he closed his eyes. "Good night, Laurie."

She doubted whether Rian heard her wish him good-night before he was asleep again.

CHAPTER NINE

A CLICK OF HEELS on the cobblestoned sun deck made Laurie open her eyes. Behind her owl-shaped sunglasses she saw Vera approaching, looking refreshingly like a spring day in a cotton dress of mint green.

"Rian said he thought you were here by the pool," the older woman greeted. "There was a phone call for you, but I couldn't find you."

"Who was it?"

"Colin. He said he would call back later."

Guiltily Laurie remembered that she had forgotten to ask Rian about the Mardi Gras Ball being held that evening. Too many things had happened since Colin had last inquired about it, although she had had several opportunities to do so. But, since the tour yesterday of Dauphin Island and the moments spent with Rian last night or rather this morning, the ball had been the last thing on her mind.

"Is Rian busy?" Laurie asked.

"He was on the telephone," Vera nodded. "I'm going into town to do some shopping. Would you like to go along? I'll be back by four o'clock and I doubt if Colin will call before then."

"No, I don't think so," Laurie refused politely. "I'd rather laze in the sun." *And think*, she added to herself.

"I don't blame you. It's a beautiful afternoon," Vera laughed, lifting her hand in goodbye. "I'll see you later."

As soon as Vera was gone, Laurie settled deeper in the wide chaise longue, adjusting her wide-brimmed white hat to keep the sun from her face. It was blissfully warm and peaceful with the gentle rays playing over her skin, bare except for the scanty covering of her yellow and blue bikini. The silence was only broken by the melodic call of the birds flitting about the outlying trees.

When Laurie had gone up to her room after leaving Rian, she had thought she would lie awake, mulling over the complications falling in love with Rian would bring into her life, but she had been asleep almost the instant her head had touched the pillow.

Before she saw him alone again, she knew she would have to decide whether she wanted to take a chance on a loveless marriage in the hope that some day Rian would grow to care for her. He had made it plain several times that he wanted a wife, implying that he would force her to marry him. More than anything else Laurie wanted to become his wife in the true sense of the word. But there was the bitter, sinking feeling that if she married him, she would become one of his possessions, something he remembered when it suited him.

Yet he wasn't completely without heart, she argued. Look at how he had helped the Trevors family. But even logic could reason that away. If Mr. Trevors was an integral part of his company, Rian would afford to do double work and pay the additional costs as long as he was certain that Arnold Trevors would recover and be back on the job in a matter of months. Gratitude had obviously made Mrs. Trevors effusive in her praise, and Laurie was quite cognizant of the charm Rian could wield when he wanted to.

No, her feelings for him would probably only amuse him or arouse his contempt for her weakness. Any declaration of how much she cared for him would be a mistake. It would never do for Rian to discover any more than that she was attracted to him as he professed to be attracted to her. But if they were married would she be able to keep her love a secret? Somehow Laurie doubted that she could. She was never one to be able to hide her feelings, especially something as searing and emotionally shaking as love.

The sound of a diver slicing into the water of the pool drew her sharply out of her reverie. A swarm of butterflies attacked her stomach, their wings beating against its walls as Laurie recognized the black-haired swimmer surfacing in the middle of the pool. She watched the sinewy muscles of his darkly tanned arms as they cleaved the water with the expert strokes of an accomplished swimmer. After swimming several lengths of the pool, Rian halted at the side nearest Laurie, his teeth flashing in a wide mocking smile as he hauled himself onto the cobblestoned edge.

The sun glinted off his wet skin, making him appear like a highly polished bronze statue. "And Lorelei sits on the rock, luring men to their destruction," he intoned cynically as he reached for the large towel on the table to wipe himself dry. "Is that what you are, Laurie? One of the sirens?"

"That description might fit LaRaine, but not me," Laurie replied with more calm than she considered possible with the taut state of her nerves.

"You underestimate your power to attract," Rian remarked, walking over to tower above her. The nakedness of his body clad in gold swimming trunks with a black stripe down the sides disturbed her more than she cared to admit. She certainly didn't underestimate his power, fighting the overwhelming desire to run her fingers through the black cloud of hairs on his chest.

"Perhaps," Laurie shrugged, closing her eyes to shut out the intoxicating sight of Rian.

Before she realized what was happening, Rian had reached down and removed her smoke-colored sunglasses. "I don't like looking at my own reflection when I'm talking to someone," he declared with infuriating complacency.

The sun's glare momentarily blinded her as she attempted to shield its rays with her hand. "The sun's in my eyes," Laurie protested.

Her glasses were placed out of reach on the chair that held his towel. Then Rian sat down on a narrow edge of Laurie's chaise longue, a hand on each

side of the back where her head rested, his lean
body effectively blocking out the glare of the sun
after he had sent her hat sailing across the sun
deck.

"Is that better?" he taunted.

"Give me back my glasses," Laurie gulped as
Rian came dangerously close. A primitive ache for
his touch throbbed through her body.

"Do you know there are times when your eyes
grow so big and round that a man feels as if he
could drown in them?" Rian murmured, ignoring
her request.

"S-stop teasing me," she stammered, catching
at the breath he was slowly stealing.

"I didn't realize that was what I was doing," he
chuckled.

"You know you're just saying those things to
get a rise out of me," Laurie declared hotly.

"Why? I've told you before that I thought you
were beautiful." A bland expression was on his
face while his eyes moved slowly over her bare
skin, sending flaming color to her cheeks. "In that
outfit, you look doubly alluring."

This conversation was unnerving Laurie. "I
think I'll take a last swim before it gets too cool."

She started to lean forward, expecting Rian to
move back and allow her to get to her feet, but he
remained where he was. She succeeded only in
drawing closer to him, finding the sensual curve of
his mouth had a hypnotic effect.

"Please let me up, Rian." The trembling in her
voice betrayed her inner awareness of him.

"Every time I start to make love to you, you run away. Why is that?" His voice was a caressing whisper. "Are you afraid you might like it?"

As Rian moved closer, Laurie sank farther back against the cushions. Her breathing became constricted as the outcome of their meeting began to seem inevitable.

"Why are you doing this?" she murmured, the agony of wanting him becoming almost more than she could bear. "I mean nothing to you."

"On the contrary, you're my fiancée." The suggestion of a jeer in his tone.

"Must you keep bringing that up?" Laurie protested weakly, her shimmering blue eyes taking in the rugged firm lines of his arrogant features. "Our engagement is a farce."

"I assure you the ring on your finger didn't come from Woolworth's, and you yourself placed it there." A wicked gleam lit his dark eyes.

"It was put there and it's stayed there for only one reason—your aunt, Vera Manning. It doesn't give you any privileges to amuse yourself with me," Laurie declared, firmly controlling her senses that cried for his touch.

"When I touch you, Laurie," Rian said quietly, "it's not in fun. I'm completely serious."

"You're twisting what I say for your own purposes!" Despair rang in her voice as she tore her gaze away from his face to study the tanned arm by her head with its darkly curling hair.

"You act as though I have some sinister designs on your virtue." Impatience lent a knife-sharp edge to his words. "I've offered you marriage."

"A marriage without love," Laurie reminded him bitterly.

"Is that so bad? Arranged marriages are still a custom in many parts of the world. They work very well. A man and a woman walk into their marriage with their eyes open and not blinded by love." The last came out as a sneer.

"But this is America!" Her gaze unwillingly returned to his face.

"May I finish it for you?" Rian mocked. "And you're not a 'Pelican girl' marrying to serve her king."

"Exactly," she breathed.

"Why? I somehow don't think my caress would be repulsive to you." The look in his eyes sent her heart hammering, occasionally skipping beats at the burning fire in their blackness.

"I don't want you to make love to me, Rian." Her statement was true because she was too afraid she might reveal the way she cared for him.

"Your lips tell me one thing, but your eyes tell me something different."

"What do my eyes tell you?" Laurie bluffed bravely. "That I think you're an arrogant and autocratic man. That you're coldly callous when it comes to the emotions of other people. Ignoring the question of how deep LaRaine's affection might have been, you pursued her, gave her expensive presents, asked her to be your wife, then tossed her off like an old shoe when an obstacle came along and cold-bloodedly replaced her with me. I pity any woman who would be foolish enough to fall in love with you. You have no compassion.''

Rian emitted a low laugh, amused by her barbs that could find no mark. ''Is that what you are afraid of? That you'll fall in love with me?'' Laurie already had and self-pity was beginning to well up inside her. ''But you've already told me that I don't possess any of the qualities you're looking for in a husband. Is that why you continue to resist me when you know you're as attracted to me as I am to you? Because you want me to be warm and tender and kind? That's a young girl's dream. You're a woman. Would you be content with a man who would cater to every whim? Do you truly want to be cuddled by a father image? Or be made love to by a man?''

His questions bombarded her and Laurie knew the answer to them all. Yes, she was in love with him. Yes, that was why she resisted him. No, she didn't want Rian to be gentle and kind, because she wanted him the way he was. She didn't want to be treated like a fragile china doll. She wanted her lips bruised by a thousand violent kisses. But she could say none of that.

''Please. . . .'' A broken sob rose in her throat, choking off any further protest.

''It's time you made up your mind, Laurie.'' Rian's head moved closer to hers, his mouth stopping a hair's breadth away from her own. ''Tell me you don't want to feel my lips against yours, or for me to nuzzle your ear and whisper love words for you alone. Shall I explore that vein on your neck that throbs so delectably rapidly when I arouse you? And your golden shoulders? The irristible hollow of your throat and the tantalizing curve of your breasts? Tell me you don't want me to do any of those things,'' he demanded in an low husky voice raw with desire that fanned an answering flame in Laurie.

With a little moan of surrender, Laurie curled her fingers around his neck, bringing his mouth onto hers as she reveled in the searing fire of his embrace. There was a complete abandonment of her carefully erected defenses, her lips parting in compliance to the demand of his. The full weight of his lean body spread over her, but she could only glory in the nakedness of their touching skin. Exploding shivers of ecstasy trembled over her until she lost all awareness of anything except Rian. The rough caress of his expert hands was ever constant—seeking, arousing, molding her soft body to the muscular contours of his.

His mouth explored her neck, first nuzzling, then nibbling at the sensitive areas until Laurie moaned from the agony of her hunger. The offending strap of her bikini was pushed aside as he caressed her shoulders, then moved to the hollow of her breasts. Rian's breathing was as ragged as hers when he returned to devour her mouth, her fingers raking the black thickness of his hair. His rising desire to possess her was becoming increasingly apparent and Laurie had long ago lost the inclination to resist.

"Rian!" E.J. Denton's voice was a blast of cold air in the blistering heat of their desire.

The curses that Rian muttered underneath his breath as he straightened, silently thrilled Laurie, still filled with the stirring knowledge of power, aware that she was able to arouse Rian as much as he aroused her.

"What is it?" he snapped.

E.J. stood hesitantly on the opposite side of the pool. "There's a telephone call for a Miss *LaRaine* Evans."

Irritation at the interruption was replaced by clinical aloofness as Rian turned his piercing dark gaze to Laurie. She hadn't missed the emphasis on her cousin's name, but she could think of no one who would be calling LaRaine. She moved her head in a negative response, her blue eyes darkening in apprehension that someone else would learn of her masquerade. Rian rose abruptly from the chaise longue, gathering up his toweling robe with a quick sweep of his hand.

"I'll handle this," he told Laurie. "You wait here."

Nearly a quarter of an hour later, Rian returned, dressed in white slacks and an unbuttoned coral shirt that intensified the blackness of his hair and the darkness of his tan. Laurie leaned anxiously forward in her lounge chair as he walked around the pool to her side, her pulse leaping in a hoped for wish to be in his arms again.

"Who was it?" she asked calmly while her senses clamored at his presence.

"False alarm," Rian answered indifferently, picking up the wraparound skirt that matched Laurie's bikini and tossing it to her. "It was Colin calling about the Mardi Gras Ball tonight."

"It completely slipped my mind," Laurie murmured, finding the mask of reserve on Rian's face difficult to penetrate. "I was supposed to ask you...."

"If I was attending," he finished for her, a cynical curl to his mouth.

"I'm sorry," she said hesitantly.

"Don't apologize. Colin explained that the arrangements were tentative, made before I arrived in Mobile, then magnanimously adjusted to include me. It was very thoughtful."

Laurie flinched at the sarcasm in his tone. "Colin has been thoughtful, escorting me to the various Mardi Gras festivities and inviting both of us to the final ball." Her awkward defense amused Rian. "He was only being kind."

"And warm and tender," he jeered.

"Will you stop bringing that up!" she snapped angrily, wrapping the skirt around her waist and securing the tie. If only she knew what had brought about the change in Rian from ardent lover to taunting stranger! "I certainly hope you had the decency to decline his invitation politely."

"Who said I declined?" An eyebrow arched contemptuously.

"Are you going?" A quick frown knitted her forehead, as she stared up at him in bewilderment.

"Have no fear, I'm not going. I told Colin that I had business to attend to."

"I don't understand then," she faltered.

"You and Colin are going alone. I certainly wouldn't want you to miss the social event of the year," he said scornfully. "I know you'll be the belle of the ball."

"You're allowing me to go with Colin?" Her eyes rounded in disbelief.

"Isn't that what I just said?"

"Yes, but...." Laurie stopped in hopeless confusion. "But you've repeatedly warned me to stay away from Colin." She wanted to say that she didn't want to go without Rian, but his coolness made such an admission impossible.

"Have I?" he asked with rhetorical indifference.

"You know you have," she retorted sharply.

"If you don't want to go, Laurie, simply call the man back and tell him," Rian snapped impatiently, his brows gathering into a threatening black cloud. "It doesn't matter to me one way or the other. Go or stay—it's up to you."

If Laurie had any question whether his attraction to her was more than physical, his freezing words answered it. "I'm going to the ball with Colin," she said quietly, salvaging a bit of her pride and independence.

"He'll pick you up at nine-thirty this evening." There was a patronizing nod of his head. "I have some telephone calls to make." And he pivoted on his heel and was gone.

Utter torment racked through her slender body at his rejection of her as anything more than a member of the opposite sex. Shivers rippled over her skin in reaction to the fluctuation of her inner body temperature that was one time hot and the other cold. Had what little attraction she held for him died when he learned she was his any time he wanted her? Had those tempestuous moments revealed her aching need for his possession of her? Rian was ruthless, autocratic, completely lacking in human compassion, her mind cried.

But with a broken sob, Laurie knew she still loved him—a hopeless, futile emotion that would only bring her heartbreak and misery. She saw that when it was too late. If Rian only returned one tenth of the love she felt for him, she would marry him. Half an hour ago, in his arms, she would have agreed without hesitation. Now a yawning void stretched ahead of her. Did its blackness hold an empty marriage to Rian or the infinity of misery and loneliness of a life without him? In her agony of loving him, Laurie couldn't decide.

Her ingrained sense of pride and self-respect prevented her from collapsing under the weight of her writhing anguish. With dogged determination, she took special interest in her appearance, resolving that Rian would never guess how much he had hurt her by palming her off on Colin for the evening.

Long preparation was taken to make herself look as stunning as possible. Laurie spent an hour in a bath full of bubbles to relax her jangled nerves. Then another hour in front of the mirror painstakingly applying her makeup. Then more time arranging her thick black hair in different styles before choosing a Grecian look with trailing white ribbonettes that added to her femininity while accentuating the pureness of her features.

Lastly she donned her evening gown, the only one she possessed, but it suited her perfectly. Gleaming white satin hung straight to the floor with the effect of a mock train at the back. Sleeveless, the neckline dipped demurely in the front and plunged in the back, complementing the golden tan of her skin. The classically simple line of the gown was highlighted by handsewn seed pearls artfully scrolled under the bodice to her slim waist. The final touch was elegant long white gloves that extended beyond her elbows.

There was a satisfied sparkle in her sapphire eyes as she studied her reflection in the mirror. No jewelry adorned the exquisite perfection of her appearance. Without vanity, Laurie acknowledged the beauty she saw, finding self-assurance that would be an effective armor.

There was a light rap on the door. "Colin is here, Laurie," Vera told her after Laurie had bade her enter. "My dear, you look lovely! You'll be the envy of every woman there. It's a pity Rian isn't free tonight. I know he would be so proud to show you off. Still, it was considerate of him to allow you to go with Colin so you wouldn't miss the festivities."

A sharp constriction in her chest at knowing the

truth to be that Rian couldn't care less whether she took part in the Mardi Gras celebration, made it impossible for Laurie to speak. She smiled her agreement at his aunt's words and reached for her beaded evening bag. She turned for one last look in the mirror.

"I'll tell Colin you'll be right down," Vera smiled.

Laurie waited a few minutes, for the first time knowing a desire to make an entrance. She had seen LaRaine do it so often that her actions were almost instinctive as she walked quietly on the thickly carpeted hall, glided silently down the stairs to the landing. There she stopped, spying Colin at the base of the stairs looking extraordinarily handsome in his evening suit while he exchanged a few words with Vera. Rian was deep in discussion with E.J. Denton several feet away near the front door. One gloved hand rested lightly on the banister post as her gaze compelled Rian to look at her. But it was Colin who noticed her first, the white of her gown catching his eyes against the background of gold flocked paper.

"My God!" Colin breathed, his hazel eyes drinking in her beauty.

"Am I very late?" Laurie smiled, noticing the way Rian's head jerked up at the sound of her voice, feeling his gaze narrow on her as she glided down the steps to Colin.

"You look absolutely ravishing!" Colin exclaimed when he had recovered from his speechlessness. "Exactly like a Greek goddess."

He captured a gloved hand and held it gently with both of his while Laurie basked in the glow of his admiration. It was the boost her ego needed. He raised her hand to his mouth, turning the palm upward to receive his kiss. She allowed her hand to linger a bit longer than was necessary before she gently withdrew it, sending a sidelong glance at Rian from beneath her lashes, but his expression was aloof and untouched by the liberties Colin had taken with his fiancée.

"Vera had told me it was a formal affair," returning her attention to Colin. "I had hoped the gown would be suitable," deliberately insinuating that she could be out of place, the way Laurie had heard her cousin do it many times before.

"Suitable!" Colin laughed, unable to take his eyes off her. "I shall be lucky to have one dance with you."

"What do you think, Rian?" Laurie purred, whirling to face him, then floating gracefully to his side. Her sapphire-bright eyes sparkled up at his aquiline face. "Do I look all right?"

"The gown is very becoming," he commented blandly, dismissing E.J. with a nod of his head.

"Is that all?" Laurie tilted her head back in a coquettish challenge, wanting him to be so moved by her radiance as to refuse to allow her to go to the ball without him.

"What do you want me to do?" His sneering voice was lowered so his words could be heard by her only. "Kiss your hand like Hartford did?"

Hurt anger flared immediately in her eyes. "Yes!" she challenged.

As her arm began to raise to force Rian into replacing Colin's caress with his own, his hand snaked out, halting her wrist after it had only moved a few inches. The pressure of his grip turned her toward Colin.

"Enjoy yourselves," Rian drawled, a mocking smile resting momentarily on Laurie's face.

"I'm sure we will," Colin nodded, his gaze quickly turning its admiring light to Laurie.

"Here, honey," Vera spoke as she draped a fur stole around Laurie's shoulders. "It might get a little cool later on. Have a nice time."

"Yes, thank you," Laurie murmured, accepting the guidance of Colin's hand as he led her toward the door.

Hot bitter tears burned the back of her eyes while a cold ache throbbed in her chest. Once Rian had said she belonged to him, but she had the impression that he had this minute given her to Colin with cynical best wishes.

Glitter and gaiety abounded as the sound of laughter, clinking iced drinks, and the music of a dance band reigned supreme at the Mardi Gras Ball, one of several being held that night. Colin was very well known, so there was a constant stream of strangers pausing to chat with him. As Colin had prophesied, Laurie never lacked a dance partner, finding she was refusing as many offers as she accepted. Still there was no enjoyment in the evening. The men, emboldened by drink, paid her fulsome compliments that meant nothing to her since they didn't come from Rian. His patrician head kept haunting her until the din around her became a nightmarish conspiracy. When Colin suggested they leave several hours later, Laurie silently sighed with gratitude.

Colin accepted her reticence during the drive home, no doubt chalking it up to the enervating evening. Laurie thanked him with as much warmth as she could for serving as her escort that evening when he had stopped the car in front of Vera's house.

"It was strictly my pleasure," he assured her.

As he helped her out of the car, Laurie was glad of the fur stole about her shoulders. The chill of the night air swept away some of her numbness and brought her senses to life. Colin took her hand at the door, raising it to his lips in a silent salute

"Have a nice night, Laurie," he murmured, hesitating as if he would like to add more before releasing her hand and stepping back.

"Good night, Colin," she answered softly, her gloved hand opening the front door. As she walked into the hallway, she heard the sound of his car engine springing to life. Quietly Laurie secured the bolt on the door and turned to tiptoe to the stairs. The silence of the house was soothing after the din of the ball and she paused to let its peace flow over her, a weary sigh breaking from her lips.

"Reflecting on all your triumphs?" Rian's voice came from the darkness near the stairs.

Her muscles constricted as Laurie stood still in

rigid surprise. The last thing she had expected was for Rian to stay up until she returned. The thought angered her after the way he had so blithely given her to Colin.

"Don't tell me you waited up for me?" she spat out sarcastically when Rian stepped out of the darkness into the dim light of the hall. "It would be touching if it weren't so revolting!"

"I hate to puncture your inflated ego when you're still reveling in your conquests." His nostrils flared in anger. "But I've been working. You could have been home hours ago for all the attention I gave to your absence."

His words stabbed at her like a saber plunging deep into her heart. "I'd quite forgotten you existed, too," Laurie answered sharply, the lie restoring some of her pride.

"I'm sure you tried to," Rian jeered.

"It wasn't too difficult," Laurie declared airily, averting her gaze so he couldn't see the pain in her eyes as she swept off the stole and walked with false confidence to the hall closet. "Colin was a *very* attentive escort."

"I don't doubt it—with Aphrodite on his arm," he murmured complacently behind her. "In mythology her Roman counterpart Venus was married to Vulcan, the god of fire."

Laurie froze for a split second before turning toward Rian with an arched smile, demurely dimpling her cheeks. "She was also purported to have indulged in a notorious intrigue with Mars."

"So she was," Rian agreed cynically. "Am I

supposed to believe that you and Colin are engaged in an intrigue behind my back?''

"Hardly behind your back. You encouraged it," she corrected.

"I find it hard to believe." A derisive chuckle emphasized his disbelief. "Colin's inbred sense of honor wouldn't allow him to take advantage of the generosity of a friend. The old Southern code of chivalry dies hard in some families. The judge wouldn't have dreamed of touching Vera once she was married even if she had invited him. It's a case of like father, like son."

"I'm afraid you don't know Colin very well," she lied. "We didn't come straight home."

The corners of his mouth curled into a mocking smile. "Liar," Rian said smoothly. "You don't have the look of a woman who's been made love to—I should know."

A crimson color filled her cheeks, then receded quickly. "Really?" she mocked. "You forget that Colin is tender."

If she had hoped to get a rise out of Rian, she failed. There wasn't a break in the arrogance indelibly etched in his lean sardonic features.

"What a pity you aren't engaged to him."

"It certainly would simplify a great many things," she agreed bitterly.

"Foremost would be our engagement party this Saturday night."

Laurie's dark head raised with a jerk. "You aren't serious!" she gasped. "You can't mean to go through with this farce?"

"I am serious, and it's no farce," Rian declared. "I told Vera to go ahead and make the necessary arrangements. We'll make a public announcement that evening to the press."

"No!" Her denial was intensified by the horrified expression in her eyes. "We've carried this mock engagement too far already. It must end."

"Our engagement ceased to be a mockery the day I arrived here and discovered your impersonation," he ground out savagely. "That same evening you agreed to wear my ring. You're my fiancée, Laurie!"

"No!" but her protest was weak.

"And you will shortly become my wife."

"But there's no love between us, Rian," she pleaded.

There was the black fury of tightly leashed violence in his eyes. "My work takes up a great deal of my time. We won't have to suffer through too many hours of each other's company."

"What if I refuse to marry you?"

"I don't intend to give you the opportunity. You've deluded everyone into believing you're madly in love with me. There isn't any way that I'm going to let you escape."

Her temples throbbed with pain as Laurie realized that the combination of Rian's domination and her love for him would certainly corner her into marrying him. With this realization came the answer to the question she had been puzzling over. As long as Rian didn't care for her she could never marry him no matter how much she loved him.

Not even the eventuality of some day bearing his child would make up for the loveless hours she'd spend in his arms. If her love for him was going to destroy her then she would rather it be without Rian around to see.

"I hate you, Rian Montgomery!" Laurie declared, brushing past him to the stairs, wishing all the while that she did.

CHAPTER TEN

HER SLEEP WAS LEADEN and Laurie awoke with her
nerves as raw and taut as the night before. The
decision had been made. At the earliest opportunity, she would leave. Rian had never asked for her
return airline ticket which was tucked away in the
bottom of her purse. It would get her back to Los
Angeles, and that was as far as Laurie was thinking at the moment. She had no doubt Rian would
stop her if he learned of her plans. The toughest
part would be to convince him that she intended to
carry on with their engagement as he had ordered.

One look at her reflection where the stark apprehension was mirrored in her eyes told Laurie it was
going to be a difficult task. The strain of her decision was visible in the harsh lines of her face. She
shuddered at the consequences if Rian should per-
ceive the reason for her haunted look, although
she seriously doubted that it would ever occur to
him that she would attempt to thwart his plans.
She had been so malleable before, agreeing to his
commands with only the briefest of protests. She
had given him no cause to believe that it would be
any different this time, and that was on her side.

Bolstered by that logical observation, Laurie

made her way down the stairs to the breakfast area dressed in a coral trouser suit that added color to her wanness and her hair hanging long and curling at the ends to add softness to the harsh lines of strain. Her stomach muscles were too tense for anything more than toast and coffee. Luckily Vera wasn't there to prompt her to eat more, the cook informing Laurie that she had already gone riding, with instructions that Laurie was to sleep as long as she wanted.

The front door opened and closed and Laurie braced herself as footsteps sounded in the hall. Reluctantly she glanced toward the open door leading from the hall to the peacock blue and gold dining room where she sat sipping the last of her coffee. The muscles of her stomach constricted tightly as she prepared herself for the sight of Rian's lean figure. But it was E.J. Denton who started to breeze past, then caught sight of Laurie and paused in the doorway.

"Good morning," he greeted brightly. "You look none the worse for all your late revelry. Did you enjoy the ball last night?"

"I had a grand time," Laurie nodded.

"Is there more coffee in the pot?"

"Nearly half full. Would you like a cup?"

"I certainly would," E.J. sighed wearily, walking into the room and taking a clean cup from the sideboard and pouring it full of black coffee. "I need a stimulant and as they say, while the cat is away, the mouse can put his feet up."

"Is Rian gone?" Laurie held her breath, not

believing that she could have that kind of luck.

"Yes. I just came back from taking him to the airport," he nodded, removing his dark-rimmed glasses to rub his eyes. "I'll be glad when Trevors is back and he can handle these minor crises."

"When will Rian be back?" averting her gaze to her empty cup so E.J. couldn't see the sudden leap of elation that had sprung into her face.

"He's booked on a return flight from Miami this evening." E.J. drained his cup and refilled it. "I'll take this with me. The correspondence and paperwork in that study must be ten feet high."

The instant she heard the study door close, Laurie hurried upstairs to her room and rummaged through her purse for the airline ticket. With the precious paper in her hand, she dialed the reservation office from the telephone on her night stand. When she hung up the receiver, her seat on the jetliner leaving that afternoon had been verified. There was ample time left to pack, write Rian a note, and catch a cab to the airport. By the time Rian returned, she would be safely in Los Angeles.

The suitcases were spread open on the bed while Laurie rushed to fill them, not the least concerned with how neatly her clothes were folded. Over an hour later, she made a last minute search of the dresser drawers and cupboards for any belongings she might have overlooked before closing the lid of the first suitcase and locking it.

"There you are, Laurie. I was look...." Vera Manning's voice trailed off as she saw the suitcases on the bed, her startled gaze rushing to Laurie's suddenly stricken expression. "You aren't leaving?"

"Yes," she whispered. Her well thought-out explanation deserted her in the face of Vera's hurt and bewildered look.

"Why?" the older woman asked. "You look as pale as a ghost, my dear. Is something wrong? Has something happened?"

Laurie gestured helplessly toward the telephone, forcing the words through the constriction in her throat. "I...I received a phone call earlier. There's been an accident. My m-mother's in the hospital. I have to fly home right away."

"Oh, my poor Laurie, no wonder you look so upset!" Vera moved quickly to her side, taking a trembling hand and placing it between her own. "Is there anything I can do?"

"I've already made my plane reservations and finished the last of my packing. I don't believe I've forgotten anything," Laurie shrugged. Her genuine agitation was a convincing if unintended ploy.

"What a time for Rian to be gone!" Vera shook her head sadly. "Do you want me to contact him? I know he'll rush right back. A man is much more able to handle emergencies like this."

"No, no, don't do that," Laurie rushed in. "I've probably made it sound more serious than it is," she continued more calmly. "The shock and all of the phone call. Mother broke a leg and suffered a mild concussion, but they assured me she wasn't in any kind of danger."

"Well, that's a relief," Vera smiled consolingly. "Naturally you want to be with her anyway to reassure yourself. I quite understand how you feel."

"It was going to write Rian a note explaining everything as soon as I'd finished packing." Laurie took a deep breath. "I probably won't be able to make it back for the engagement party you'd planned for this weekend."

"Don't give it another thought," Vera ordered. "It was a spur-of-the-moment idea anyway. Our friends will understand why it has to be canceled. It's nearly lunch time. Would you like some soup or a sandwich to settle your stomach? Carla said you only had toast for breakfast."

"I really couldn't eat a thing. I'm sure they'll serve a snack on the plane if I should get hungry later."

"I'll send Sam up for your bags. He'll drive you to the airport whenever you want to leave. Everything will turn out just fine, Laurie."

"Oh, Vera," her chin trembled traitorously. "You've been so good to me. I hate to leave like this." The warmhearted woman made Laurie wish she had stolen out in the middle of the night rather than deceive Vera again with more lies.

"So do I," Vera nodded, a shimmering of tears in her own blue eyes. "But we neither one of us had any control over it, did we?"

After Vera had left, Laurie sat down and composed the note to Rian. She kept the message terse, not allowing her heartache at leaving him to be revealed as she told him that she was leaving and in no circumstances would she ever consent to marrying him, that he might as well take her decision as final and not attempt to follow her. She placed it, the sapphire engagement ring, and the bracelet in Rian's bedroom, telling Vera that she had left his note there.

Two hours later Laurie was on board the plane streaking across the sky toward Los Angeles. But she didn't draw a secure breath until her luggage was stowed in a taxicab at the airport and she had climbed in the rear seat, giving the address of the apartment she shared with LaRaine to the cab driver. She had forgotten how little money she had with her until they reached her destination and she had to spend nearly all of it to pay the fare.

Asking the driver to carry the bags inside the lobby of the building, Laurie walked through the glass doors. Her expression curved into a weary but happy smile as she saw that her security friend, Tom Farber, was on duty.

"How are you today, Mr. Farber?" she greeted.

"Well, you sure are a sight for sore eyes. What are you doing back here?" he grinned. "Not that I'm not glad to see you, because I am."

"Why shouldn't I be back?" Laurie asked, a puzzled frown on her forehead. "I live here."

An apprehensive mask stole over his face. "I thought something was wrong," he said hesitantly. "I'm sorry, Miss Evans, but your cousin canceled her lease on the apartment and moved out a week ago."

"You must be mistaken!" she gasped.

"She left her parents' address to forward her mail to and said you wouldn't be back," Tom Farber nodded grimly. "Perhaps you should call your aunt."

"Yes, yes, I'd better," Laurie agreed absently, taken aback by the discovery that she had no place to stay.

"You're welcome to use the phone here," he offered, motioning to the phone on the counter.

With a dreadful feeling of unease, Laurie dialed the number of her cousin's parents. The phone was answered on the second ring, and she immediately recognized the voice of her aunt.

"Aunt Carrie, this is Laurie," but she got no further than that.

"I didn't think you'd have the nerve to call here," her aunt's shrill voice declared. "After what you did to poor LaRaine, I'm surprised you'd even dare to show your face!"

"After what I did to LaRaine?" Laurie echoed.

"Yes! My poor baby was just torn apart when she discovered how you'd stolen her fiancé right from under her nose, without a care of how badly her heart was broken. And to think of the way your uncle and I sacrificed to raise you as our own and to have you pay us back like this! It's horrible!"

"You didn't have to sacrifice," Laurie's chin trembled as she was near to tears. "My father left enough money to take care of me."

"And you squandered that, too!" Carrie Evans cried. "Well, don't think we're going to support you any more! Get your wealthy fiancé to take care of you, and stay out of our lives! You've done enough damage already!"

And the line was dead. Her aunt had hung up on her. It was obvious that LaRaine hadn't told her parents the truth about how Laurie had happened to be in Mobile instead of her. Heaven only knew what spiteful lies her cousin had told after Rian had terminated their engagement. But the end result was that her aunt and uncle wanted nothing more to do with her.

The full weight of her predicament sagged her shoulders as she turned her lost expression toward the sympathetic face of the uniformed guard.

"They tossed you out on your ear, did they?" he said gruffly, a pain twisting in his chest at the glumly resigned nod of the blue black head.

"What am I going to do?" Laurie sighed, then gave a bitter laugh. "I don't even have enough money for a place to stay tonight."

"I could lend you some," he offered gently.

"No, no, I couldn't let you do that," she protested with a sad and firm shake of her head. "I'll get by."

"Would you consider the offer of a place to sleep tonight?" hurrying on before Laurie had a chance to interrupt. "My wife and I have a real nice guest bedroom in our home. It wouldn't be any trouble at all and it would give you a place to stay until you decide what you're going to do."

"I know what I'm going to do. I'm going to get a job," Laurie smiled weakly. "But I really wouldn't feel right about taking any more charity." The harsh words of her aunt were still ringing in her mind.

"It wouldn't be charity," Tom Farber insisted with a perceptive understanding of the reason behind her refusal. "As soon as you find yourself a job, you could pay us whatever you felt was fair for your board and room." It was a very tempting offer, but Laurie hesitated. "Tell you what, you think it over," he smiled. "Sit down here on the couch, have a cup of coffee and relax. Ed Jenkins will be here in about fifteen minutes to relieve me so I can go home. If you decide you want to leave, I'll give you a lift wherever you want. If you want to come home with me, then that would be just great. How about it?"

"I'll agree to that suggestion, Mr. Farber." His cajoling expression coaxed her into a genuine smile.

"It's Tom to my friends."

"And Laurie to mine," she smiled, taking the hand he held out to her.

A quarter of an hour later, Tom Farber was loading her red luggage into the trunk of his car. Of the two alternatives he had offered her, only the one was sensible—to stay with Tom and his wife. Laurie refused to consider the third possibility of contacting Rian. As much as she loved him, she would rather starve than marry him when he didn't love her.

When Tom crawled behind the wheel of the car, Laurie glanced hesitantly at his cheerful face.

"Tom," she began, then paused to phrase her words, "if someone should come looking for me at the apartment, could you. . .would you tell them you don't know where I am?" If Rian did come looking for her, Laurie wanted to be sure he couldn't find her and manage to charm her into marriage.

"Are you in some kind of trouble?" he probed gently.

"No, not really. There's a man who might want to speak to me, but I don't want to see him," Laurie replied in a tight voice.

"Then he'll never find out where you are from me," Tom declared with a wink.

Betty Farber, Tom's wife, turned out to be as warm and friendly as her husband, shooing away Laurie's apologies for disrupting their household and declaring she would be glad of a woman around the house to gossip with. Exhausted by her hurried flight from Mobile, hurt by the rejection of her aunt and uncle, Laurie had trouble sleeping that night. Her mind insisted on reliving each memory of the moments spent with Rian, the tortuous knowledge that she must never see him again adding unbearable pain. Her pillow was damp when she finally fell asleep.

The next day Betty insisted that Laurie needed to rest up from her trip, allowing her to do no more than circle advertisements for help wanted. Despite the woman's perpetually gay chatter, Laurie felt the hours dragging by and wondered how she would ever get through a lifetime without Rian.

At the supper table that evening, Tom Farber eyed her curiously, taking in the slightly puffy eyelids, the dullness of her expression, and the absence of her usually ready smile. When the dessert had been consumed and the coffee cups were in front of them, he cleared his throat. Blank blue eyes glanced up at him in a reflex action.

"Were you referring to that Montgomery man yesterday?" he asked, masking his interest to stare at his cup.

"Was he at the apartment?" A piercing sadness mixed with the apprehension in her expression as Laurie avoided a direct answer.

Tom nodded, "Yes, he was. At first I thought he was looking for LaRaine and I told him she'd moved back with her parents. But he quickly put me straight in no uncertain terms that he was looking for you."

"What did you tell him?" she whispered, imagining the thwarted anger that must have driven Rian to make him fly all the way to Los Angeles to find her.

"The truth, but not the whole truth. I said you arrived at the apartment yesterday afternoon, discovered your cousin had dropped the lease, made a telephone call, and left."

"Did he believe you?"

"I think so," the man nodded. "He said you were his fiancée."

Laurie blanched, her fingers touching the faintly white circle where the sapphire ring had adorned her hand. "I was, but it's all over."

A silent message was exchanged between husband and wife that Laurie missed and the subject was deftly changed to some inconsequential happening that didn't require her attention. A few minutes later she mumbled a request to be excused and walked swiftly to her room, where not even the shedding of tears could assuage the twisting agonizing pain in her heart.

After only a few days of job hunting, Laurie had her application accepted for an opening in the typing pool of a large firm of attorneys. Concentrating on the awkward legal jargon kept her attention centered on her work, and forced the haunting images of Rian to the recesses of her mind. The daylight hours passed swiftly during the week, without the agonizing cruelty of the nights and the empty loneliness of the weekends. But the ache remained, striking with piercing swiftness as an odd word would bring back some memory with vivid clarity, or throbbing in the background becoming a part of her existence like the beat of her heart.

Never once in three months did Tom or Betty Farber bring up the subject of her broken engagement, and Laurie couldn't talk about it, either. The first month after she had gone to work, she had made a half-hearted attempt to find an apartment. Few were in the price range that her meager salary could support. The prospect of sharing an apartment with another girl didn't appeal to her, either. And Betty and Tom were so set against her going out on her own that Laurie finally gave in and agreed to stay on with them.

One Monday evening after the supper dishes were done, Laurie sat at the oval dining room table, leafing haphazardly through the newspaper. A photograph leaped out at her from the top of the page freezing her into immobility as she stared at the virile dark-haired man in the center of the picture. The blur of the newspaper photograph didn't hide the arrogant set of Rian Montgomery's head as he gazed down at the girl at his side. Unwillingly Laurie shifted her attention to the dark-haired girl provocatively glancing up at him. It was LaRaine, her cousin!

Swallowing back the sob that bubbled in her throat, Laurie read the caption beneath the picture. "Hotel owner and entrepreneur Rian Montgomery was seen escorting the rising young newcomer LaRaine Evans at a recent Hollywood party. Rumor has it there's a dark-haired fiancée in Rian's life. Could this be the one?"

Laurie tried to be glad that Rian and LaRaine had got back together. She tried, but she kept remembering the way his dark eyes looked at her, probing, searching, sparking that flame of desire that punctuated the times they spent together. All those memories that she had fought so hard to push to the back of her mind came racing back. It might as well have been yesterday that she had left him, so sharp and fresh was the pain of her love. Laurie didn't even realize she was crying until she saw the wet drops smearing the newspaper print. A hand to her cheeks verified their wetness. Quickly she scrubbed the tears away, closed the paper, and walked to her room, not noticing the questioning gaze from the man in the easy chair.

LAURIE'S POWERS OF CONCENTRATION had deserted her. Liberal use of cover stick makeup hid the dark circles, evidence of a trio of sleepless nights. Tired blue eyes skimmed the page Laurie had just typed, despair crying out at her inability to tolerate the remotest introduction of Rian's name in her life as she realized she had typed his name in place of the party's name that belonged in the legal document. The glaring error could not be corrected. The entire page had to be done over again, and Laurie wanted to weep in frustration as she removed the paper and its carbons from the typewriter.

Footsteps sounded beside her desk and Laurie cringed in anticipation of Mr. Jennings' wrath when he discovered the document was not completed. A quick apology formed on her lips.

"I'm sorry, I haven't finished it yet. I only have one page left...." The apologetic words died in her throat as Laurie glanced up. Her mind was playing tricks on her, making her see Rian's face when he wasn't even there. She blinked once, then again, but he didn't go away.

"Hello, Laurie," Rian said grimly, obsidian dark eyes staring at her with unrelenting harshness.

"What are you doing here?" she whispered. She glanced around anxiously, seeing the interested looks on the faces of the other girls in the room.

"I should think it would be obvious," his cruel voice jeered.

Her senses were undergoing a terrible upheaval. Laurie wasn't able to meet his mockingly severe look and turned to stare at her typewriter. "Go away, Rian." It was more than she could bear to have him so close to her and not want to be in his arms.

"The game of hide and seek is over," he declared viciously.

"Please, leave me alone," she begged in a whispering voice that threatened to break.

"Miss Evans, do you have that agreement typed yet?" A harried man with disheveled hair came bustling to her desk, his preoccupied air preventing him from noticing the tall imposing man standing there as well.

"Not yet, Mr. Jennings," Laurie answered tightly.

"I need it immediately."

"Would you mind," Rian interrupted with the autocratic ease of one accustomed to making others wait. "I'm speaking to the young lady."

"See here . . ." her employer began indignantly, turning an outraged face toward Rian, only for the expression to slowly recede as he met the full force of the arrogantly set gaze. "Aren't you . . ." Mr. Jennings began.

"Montgomery, Rian Montgomery," he supplied without the barest glimmer of remorse for his usurping of Laurie.

"Of course, I thought I recognized you," Mr.

Jennings smiled, his pale eyes lighting up at the name. "What can we do for you, Mr. Montgomery?"

"I'd like to talk to Miss Evans alone. Somewhere private." Rian ignored the gasp of dismay that came from Laurie.

"Miss Evans?" the man repeated blankly, gazing down at her as though he had forgotten she was there. "Yes, of course," he stumbled briefly. "There's an office right over here you can use."

The dark gaze rested on Laurie again, challenging her to refuse to see him alone. That was exactly what she wanted to do. The shock of seeing him again after so many months had shattered her defenses. He read the hesitation in her eyes, the half-formed decision to protest.

"Would you prefer to have our discussion take place here?" Rian asked, a derisive glance encompassing the roomful of women. "In front of an audience?"

Reluctantly Laurie rose from her chair, surprised to find her legs were capable of supporting her, and followed Mr. Jennings to the office two doors down the hall from the typing pool. Rian followed her, anticipating her desire to bolt and successfully shutting off her escape.

Inside the office with the door closed behind them, Laurie glanced anxiously toward Rian, thinking his features had grown more forbidding and cynically withdrawn. His long stride carried him to the window where the sunlight streaming in threw his face into the shadows.

"Did you truly think I wouldn't find you, Laurie?" he asked contemptuously.

"I didn't think you would try," Laurie edged the softness of her voice.

"Didn't you? Then why did you take such pains to cover your tracks?" Rian demanded.

"I didn't...or at least, not deliberately," she amended lamely. "I returned directly to the apartment, then discovered that LaRaine had moved out. I didn't have any money, so when Tom—Mr. Farber—offered to rent me a room with him and his wife, I accepted."

"Then made sure he told no one where you were. Too bad the second guard, Jenkins, wasn't so closemouthed. Your aunt and uncle were half out of their minds with worry about you." His scathing retort lashed out at her already tender nerves.

"That's a lie! Aunt Carrie told me not to set foot...." Her angry words died at the sudden glint that appeared in Rian's dark eyes. "It doesn't matter," she shrugged, then hugged her arms about her to stem the churning of her stomach. "Why did you have to come looking for me? Why couldn't you have left me alone?"

"You're my fiancée." There was uncompromising hardness in his expression and tone.

"Not anymore," Laurie denied fervently, lifting her hand, bare without the sapphire. "I'm not wearing your ring. I put it on and I took it off. There isn't anymore engagement."

"Only in your eyes. You left my aunt with the

mpression that you were nursing your sick
nother. There was no mention to her of any
oroken engagement," he sneered.

"How could I?" Laurie flashed. "What was I to
do? Tell her that I hated her nephew?"

"So you left it to me. I know this will be a revolting discovery to you, but Vera still believes
we're engaged." His mouth curved into a sarcastic
smile.

"Is that why you've gone to such lengths to find
me? So you can rub my nose into the mess I made
of things with my masquerade? You have no idea
how much I regret the day I arrived in Mobile!"
Her statement ended in a choked sob.

"No doubt your return trip will be just as regret-
table."

"I'm not going back," Laurie retorted.

"Oh, yes, you are," Rian rasped out harshly.
"Vera wants you to be at her wedding!"

"Wedding? Do you mean. . . . Is she marrying
the judge?" A tiny glow of happiness brought a
sparkle to her jewel eyes.

"Yes," with a savage snap. "And she expects
my *fiancée* to be there."

There was a small pause as Laurie wished secretly that she could be there as a friend. "It's impossible," she said aloud, knowing she could never
stand up under the prolonged strain of being with
Rian and not letting him see she loved him. "Take
LaRaine. It's time she met your family anyway."

"LaRaine be damned! It's you that Vera is expecting!"

"Make up a story or tell the truth," Laurie pleaded, her feet involuntarily carrying her closer to him. "We just can't keep up this pretense any longer."

"There was no pretense." The shadows no longer hid his face and the piercing glare of his gaze unnerved her. "I offered you marriage."

"Yes, but marriage without any feelings between us," she protested. Not until she saw the sudden tightening of his jaw did she realize her hands were resting against his chest in a beseeching gesture. They fluttered quickly to her side as the silence pounded as loudly as her heart.

"There was always something between us." Rian's voice vibrated with barely controlled violence. The glitter in the depths of his eyes compelled her to meet his gaze even as Laurie tore herself away, more shaken by his steel-hard magnetism than was safe.

"No." The tiny word of denial severed the thread that had held Rian in check.

The iron grip of his fingers closed over her throat, the brutal pressure pulling her against the hardness of his lean body. Yet there was no fear in her blue eyes as she gazed with aching desire into the savage brilliance of his forbidding face.

"I could kill you for the hell you've put me through," Rian snarled. His gaze moved possessively over her face. There was the slightest lessening of the pressure of his fingers around her throat. His thumb rhythmically massaged the pulsating cord in her neck, his touch so sensually arousing that Laurie's eyelashes fluttered down to hide the heat waves he was sending through her. "You've haunted my days and possessed my nights until you've nearly driven me crazy with wanting you," he declared hoarsely. "And then you say there was nothing between us."

His mouth closed over hers with punishing thoroughness. The glorious words Laurie had just heard were still ringing in her ears as she managed to return his kiss with equal fervor despite the fury that drove him to hurt. In the next moment she was crushed against his chest, Rian's lips burying themselves in the dark cloud of her hair.

"I won't let you go, Laurie," he vowed hungrily. "I can't let you go! You're mine and, God help me, I can't live without you!"

"Rian, Rian," she whispered, her whole being erupting with unbelievable happiness as she uncaringly bestowed kisses on his expertly tailored jacket concealing the heart that was thudding as wildly as hers beneath the expensive material. "Are you telling me you love me?" she asked breathlessly.

"Yes," he groaned bitterly. "Yes, I love you. I worship you. The first time I touched you at the pool when I thought you were LaRaine something strange happened to me. I blamed the violence I felt on your deceit. But I kept wanting to touch you again, to hold you in my arms and destroy you the way you were slowly destroying me."

"Rian, stop!" Laurie cried, unable to bear the bitter torment in his voice any longer. But his hand closed over her mouth, halting any words of love she wanted to say.

"Doesn't it amuse you?" he sneered, staring down into her agonized expression. "Surely the taste of victory is sweet to know that you've brought Rian Montgomery to his knees!"

Mutely she shook her head in denial.

One moment Laurie was crushed against him, in the next she was free and Rian was standing with his back to her staring out the curtained window, wearily rubbing his hand along the back of his neck.

"Will you come to Mobile with me?" he asked quietly.

"I'll go to the North Pole with you, darling," she answered just as quietly.

There was a moment of stillness when Rian froze at her words, then he pivoted swiftly around, staring at her in stunned disbelief. "What did you say?" torment in his dark, proud eyes as he braced himself for her retraction.

"I said I love you, Rian Montgomery," Laurie replied, letting all her pent up emotion shine for him alone. Then she was gliding into his arms, to be locked in a possessive embrace, returning the fire of his kiss with the white-hot flames of her own.

A considerable amount of time later, Rian held her away from him, withdrawing a cigarette from his pocket and lighting it with shaking fingers.

"As much as I would like to see you walking down the aisle of a church to me, I think we'd better get married before we fly back to Mobile," he decreed.

"Yes, Rian," Laurie agreed meekly, wrapped in the searing knowledge that he loved her.

"Laurie, why did you leave?" Even as he asked the question, his dark eyes were possessively exploring her face, reassuring himself of the love that glowed there for him.

"Because I thought you didn't care for me," she answered honestly, only now realizing how wrong she had been. "You kept saying I had to marry you, yet you so callously pawned me off on Colin that.... If you loved me then, Rian, why did you put me in a position of being forced to go to the ball with him?"

He inhaled deeply before answering. "That time at the pool before Colin called—do you remember?" A crimson blush filled Laurie's cheeks as she remembered very vividly how abandonedly she had responded to Rian. "Yes, well," he continued, "you may believe this or not, but that was the first time I'd ever lost control when I was making love to a woman. If E.J. hadn't come out when he did...." His gaze raked over her, knowing she had filled in the rest. "I fully realized then what was happening and like any normal red-blooded male, I bolted. I wasn't going to let any woman put a ring through my nose."

That statement drew a lilting laugh from Laurie at the incongruous thought that Rian could ever be led.

"What about that photograph in the newspaper

of you and LaRaine? I thought you'd gone back to her.'' Sobering as she remembered the pain she had felt.

"I was trying to find you, darling. That was the only reason I saw her. Jealousy is a terrible thing, Laurie. I wanted you to go with Colin that night to prove that you meant nothing to me. It was the most agonizing night I've ever spent, except perhaps for these months when I didn't know where you were.''

"I'll never leave you," she vowed, seeking the warmth of his embrace. "Not ever again.''

"I won't let you," Rian murmured against her mouth.